The Prelimin[ary]
and Other St[ories]

Cornelia A. P. Comer

Alpha Editions

This edition published in 2024

ISBN 9789362093264

Design and Setting By
Alpha Editions
www.alphaedis.com
Email - info@alphaedis.com

As per information held with us this book is in Public Domain.
This book is a reproduction of an important historical work.
Alpha Editions uses the best technology to reproduce historical work
in the same manner it was first published to preserve its original nature.
Any marks or number seen are left intentionally to preserve.

Contents

I .... - 1 -

II .... - 4 -

III .... - 8 -

IV .... - 12 -

THE LONG INHERITANCE .... - 18 -

I .... - 19 -

II .... - 23 -

III .... - 29 -

IV .... - 34 -

V .... - 36 -

VI .... - 39 -

CLARISSA'S OWN CHILD .... - 46 -

I .... - 47 -

II .... - 54 -

III .... - 62 -

IV .... - 66 -

I

Young Oliver Pickersgill was in love with Peter Lannithorne's daughter. Peter Lannithorne was serving a six-year term in the penitentiary for embezzlement.

It seemed to Ollie that there was only one right-minded way of looking at these basal facts of his situation. But this simple view of the matter was destined to receive several shocks in the course of his negotiations for Ruth Lannithorne's hand. I say negotiations advisedly. Most young men in love have only to secure the consent of the girl and find enough money to go to housekeeping. It is quite otherwise when you wish to marry into a royal family, or to ally yourself with a criminal's daughter. The preliminaries are more complicated.

Ollie thought a man ought to marry the girl he loves, and prejudices be hanged! In the deeps of his soul, he probably knew this to be the magnanimous, manly attitude, but certainly there was no condescension in his outward bearing when he asked Ruth Lannithorne to be his wife. Yet she turned on him fiercely, bristling with pride and tense with overwrought nerves.

"I will never marry any one," she declared, "who does n't respect my father as I do!"

If Oliver's jaw fell, it is hardly surprising. He had expected her to say she would never marry into a family where she was not welcome. He had planned to get around the natural objections of his parents somehow--the details of this were vague in his mind--and then he meant to reassure her warmly, and tell her that personal merit was the only thing that counted with him or his. He may have visualized himself as wiping away her tears and gently raising her to share the safe social pedestal whereon the Pickersgills were firmly planted. The young do have these visions not infrequently. But to be asked to respect Peter Lannithorne, about whom he knew practically nothing save his present address!

"I don't remember that I ever saw your father, Ruth," he faltered.

"He was the best man," said the girl excitedly, "the kindest, the most indulgent--that's another thing, Ollie. I will never marry an indulgent man, nor one who will let his wife manage him. If it had n't been for mother--" She broke off abruptly.

Ollie tried to look sympathetic and not too intelligent. He had heard that Mrs. Lannithorne was considered difficult.

"I ought n't to say it, but can't explain father unless I do. Mother nagged; she wanted more money than there was; she made him feel her illnesses, and our failings, and the overdone beefsteak, and the underdone bread,-- everything that went wrong, always, was his fault. His fault--because he did n't make more money. We were on the edge of things, and she wanted to be in the middle, as she was used to being. Of course, she really has n't been well, but I think it's mostly nerves," said Ruth, with the terrible hardness of the young. "Anyhow, she might just as well have stuck knives into him as to say the things she did. It hurt him--like knives. I could see him wince-- and try harder--and get discouraged--and then, at last " The girl burst into a passion of tears.

Oliver tried to soothe her. Secretly he was appalled at these squalid revelations of discordant family life. The domestic affairs of the Pickersgills ran smoothly, in affluence and peace. Oliver had never listened to a nagging woman in his life. He had an idea that such phenomena were confined to the lower classes.

"Don't you care for me at all, Ruth?"

The girl crumpled her wet handkerchief. "Ollie, you're the most beautiful thing that ever happened except my father. He was beautiful, too; indeed, indeed, he was. I'll never think differently. I can't. He tried so hard."

All the latent manliness in the boy came to the surface and showed itself.

"Ruth, darling, I don't want you to think differently. It's right for you to be loyal and feel as you do. You see, you know, and the world doesn't. I'll take what you say and do as you wish. You must n't think I'm on the other side. I'm not. I'm on your side, wherever that is. When the time comes I'll show you. You may trust me, Ruth."

He was eager, pleading, earnest. He looked at the moment so good, so loving and sincere, that the girl, out of her darker experience of life, wondered wistfully if it were really true that Providence ever let people just live their lives out like that being good, and prosperous, and generous, advancing from happiness to happiness, instead of stubbing along painfully as she felt she had done, from one bitter experience to another, learning to live by failures.

It must be beautiful to learn from successes instead, as it seemed to her Oliver had done. How could any one refuse to share such a radiant life when it was offered? As for loving Oliver, that was a foregone conclusion. Still, she hesitated.

"You re awfully dear and good to me, Ollie," she said. "But I want you to see father. I want you to go and talk to him about this, and know him for yourself. I know I'm asking a hard thing of you, but, truly, I believe it's best. If *he* says it's all right for me to marry you, I will if your family want me, of course," she added as an after thought.

"Ought n't I to speak to your mother?" hesitated Oliver.

"Oh,--mother? Yes, I suppose she'd like it," said Ruth absent-mindedly. "Mother has views about getting married, Ollie. I dare say she'll want to tell you what they are. You must n't think they're my views, though."

"I'd rather hear yours, Ruth."

She flashed a look at him that opened for him the heavenly deeps that lie before the young and the loving, and he had a sudden vision of their life as a long sunlit road, winding uphill, winding down, but sunlit always--because looks like that illumine any dusk.

"I'll tell you my views--some day," Ruth said softly. "But first--"

"First I must talk to my father, your mother, your father." Oliver checked them off on his fingers. "Three of them. Seems to me that's a lot of folks to consult about a thing that does n't really concern anybody but you and me!"

II

After the fashion of self-absorbed youth, Oliver had never noticed Mrs. Lannithorne especially. She had been to him simply a sallow little figure in the background of Ruth's vivid young life; some one to be spoken to very politely, but otherwise of no particular moment.

If his marital negotiations did nothing else for him, they were at least opening his eyes to the significance of the personalities of older people.

The things Ruth said about her mother had prepared him to find that lady querulous and difficult, but essentially negligible. Face to face with Mrs. Lannithorne, he had a very different impression. She received him in the upstairs sitting-room to which her semi-invalid habits usually confined her. Wrapped in a white wool shawl and lying in a long Canton lounging-chair by a sunshiny window, she put out a chilly hand in greeting, and asked the young man to be seated.

Oliver, scanning her countenance, received an unexpected impression of dignity. She was thin and nervous, with big dark eyes peering out of a pale, narrow face; she might be a woman with a grievance, but he apprehended something beyond mere fretfulness in the discontent of her expression. There was suffering and thought in her face, and even when the former is exaggerated and the latter erroneous, these are impressive things.

"Mrs. Lannithorne, have you any objection to letting Ruth marry me?"

"Mr. Pickersgill, what are your qualifications for the care of a wife and family?"

Oliver hesitated. "Why, about what anybody's are, I think," he said, and was immediately conscious of the feebleness of this response. "I mean," he added, flushing to the roots of his blond hair, "that my prospects in life are fair. I am in my father's office, you know. I am to have a small share in the business next year. I need n't tell you that the firm is a good one. If you want to know about my qualifications as a lawyer why, I can refer you to people who can tell you if they think I am promising."

"Do your family approve of this marriage?"

"I have n't talked to them about it yet."

"Have you ever saved any money of your own earning, or have you any property in your own name?"

Oliver thought guiltily of his bank account, which had a surprising way of proving, when balanced, to be less than he expected.

"Well,--not exactly."

"In other words, then, Mr. Pickersgill, you are a young and absolutely untried man; you are in your father's employ and practically at his mercy; you propose a great change in your life of which you do not know that he approves; you have no resources of your own, and you are not even sure of your earning capacity if your father's backing were withdrawn. In these circumstances you plan to double your expenses and assume the whole responsibility of another person's life, comfort, and happiness. Do you think that you have shown me that your qualifications are adequate?"

All this was more than a little disconcerting. Oliver was used to being accepted as old Pickersgill's only son which meant a cheerfully accorded background of eminence, ability, and comfortable wealth. It had not occurred to him to detach himself from that background and see how he looked when separated from it. He felt a little angry, and also a little ashamed of the fact that he did not bulk larger as a personage, apart from his environment. Nevertheless, he answered her question honestly.

"No, Mrs. Lannithorne, I don't think that I have."

She did not appear to rejoice in his discomfiture. She even seemed a little sorry for it, but she went on quietly:--

"Don't think I am trying to prove that you are the most ineligible young man in the city. But it is absolutely necessary that a man should stand on his own feet, and firmly, before he undertakes to look after other lives than his own. Otherwise there is nothing but misery for the women and children who depend upon him. It is a serious business, getting married."

"I begin to think it is," muttered Oliver blankly.

"I don't **want** my daughters to marry," said Mrs. Lannithorne. "The life is a thousand times harder than that of the self-supporting woman --harder work, fewer rewards, less enjoyment, less security. That is true even of an ordinarily happy marriage. And if they are not happy --oh, the bitterness of them!"

She was speaking rapidly now, with energy, almost with anguish. Oliver, red in the face, subdued, but eager to refute her out of the depths and heights of his inexperience, held him self rigidly still and listened.

"Did you ever hear that epigram of Disraeli--that all men should marry, but no women? That is what I believe! At least, if women must marry, let others do it, not my children, not my little girls!--It is curious, but that is how we always think of them. When they are grown they are often uncongenial. My daughter Ruth does not love me deeply, nor am I greatly drawn to her now, as an individual, a personality,--but Ruth was such a dear baby! I can't bear to have her suffer."

Oliver started to protest, hesitated, bit his lip, and subsided. After all, did he dare say that his wife would never suffer? The woman opposite looked at him with hostile, accusing eyes, as if he incarnated in his youthful person all the futile masculinity in the world.

"Do you think a woman who has suffered willingly gives her children over to the same fate?" she demanded passionately. "I wish I could make you see it for five minutes as I see it, you, young, careless, foolish. Why, you know nothing,--nothing! Listen to me. The woman who marries gives up everything: or at least jeopardizes everything: her youth, her health, her life perhaps, certainly her individuality. She acquires the permanent possibility of self-sacrifice. She does it gladly, but she does not know what she is doing. In return, is it too much to ask that she be assured a roof over her head, food to her mouth, clothes to her body? How many men marry without being sure that they have even so much to offer? You yourself, of what are you sure? Is your arm strong? Is your heart loyal? Can you shelter her soul as well as her body? I know your father has money. Perhaps you can care for her creature needs, but that is n't all. For some women life is one long affront, one slow humiliation. How do I know you are not like that?"

"Because I'm not, that's all!" said Oliver Pickersgill abruptly, getting to his feet.

He felt badgered, baited, indignant, yet he could not tell this frail, excited woman what he thought. There were things one did n't say, although Mrs. Lannithorne seemed to ignore the fact. She went on ignoring it.

"I know what you are thinking," she said, "that I would regard these matters differently if I had married another man. That is not wholly true. It is because Peter Lannithorne was a good man at heart, and tried to play the man's part as well as he knew how, and because it was partly my own fault that he failed so miserably, that I have thought of it all so much. And the end of all my thinking is that I don't want my daughters to marry."

Oliver was white now, and a little unsteady. He was also confused. There was the note of truth in what she said, but he felt that she said it with too much excitement, with too great facility. He had the justified masculine distrust of feminine fluency as hysterical. Nothing so presented could carry full conviction. And he felt physically bruised and battered, as if he had been beaten with actual rods instead of stinging words; but he was not yet defeated.

"Mrs. Lannithorne, what do you wish me to understand from all this? Do you forbid Ruth and me to marry--is that it?"

She looked at him dubiously. She felt so fiercely the things she had been saying that she could not feel them continuously. She, too, was exhausted.

Oliver Pickersgill had a fine head, candid eyes, a firm chin, strong capable hands. He was young, and the young know nothing, but it might be that there was the making of a man in him. If Ruth must marry, perhaps him as well as another. But she did not trust her own judgment, even of such hands, such eyes, and such a chin. Oh, if the girls would only believe her, if they would only be content to trust the wisdom she had distilled from the bitterness of life! But the young know nothing, and believe only the lying voices in their own hearts!

"I wish you would see Ruth's father," she said suddenly. "I am prejudiced. I ought not to have to deal with these questions. I tell you, I pray Heaven none of them may marry--ever; but, just the same, they will! Go ask Peter Lannithorne if he thinks his daughter Ruth has a fighting chance for happiness as your wife. Let him settle it. I have told you what I think. I am done."

"I shall be very glad to talk with Ruth's father about the matter," said Oliver with a certain emphasis on ***father***. "Perhaps he and I shall be able to understand each other better. Good morning, Mrs. Lannithorne!"

III

Oliver Pickersgill Senior turned his swivel-chair about, bit hard on the end of his cigar, and stared at his only son.

"What's that?" he said abruptly, "Say that again."

Oliver Junior winced, not so much at the words as at his father's face.

"I want to marry Ruth Lannithorne," he repeated steadily.

There was a silence. The elder Pickersgill looked at his son long and hard from under lowered brows. Oliver had never seen his father look at him like that before: as if he were a rank outsider, some detached person whose doings were to be scrutinized coldly and critically, and judged on their merits. It is a hard hour for a beloved child when he first sees that look in heretofore indulgent parental eyes. Young Oliver felt a weight at his heart, but he sat the straighter, and did not flinch before the appraising glance.

"So you want to marry Peter Lannithorne's daughter, do you? Well, now, what is there in the idea of marrying a jail-bird's child that you find especially attractive?"

"Of course I might say that I've seen something of business men in this town, Ross, say, and Worcester, and Jim Stone, and that, if it came to a choice between their methods and Lannithorne's, his were the squarer, for he settled up, and is paying the price besides. But I don't know that there's any use saying that. I don't want to marry any of their daughters and you wouldn't want me to. You know what Ruth Lannithorne is as well as I do. If there's a girl in town that's finer-grained, or smarter, or prettier, I'd like to have you point her out! And she has a sense of honor like a man's. I don't know another girl like her in that. She knows what's fair," said the young man.

Mr. Pickersgill's face relaxed a little. Oliver was making a good argument with no mushiness about it, and he had a long-settled habit of appreciating Ollie's arguments.

"She knows what's fair, does she? Then what does she say about marrying you?"

"She says she won't marry anybody who doesn't respect her father as she does!"

At this the parent grinned a little, grimly it is true, but appreciatively. He looked past Oliver's handsome, boyish head, out of the window, and was silent for a time. When he spoke, it was gravely, not angrily.

"Oliver, you're young. The things I'm as sure of as two and two, you don't yet believe at all. Probably you won't believe 'em if I put them to you, but it's up to me to do it. Understand, I'm not getting angry and doing the heavy father over this. I'm just telling you how some things are in this world,--facts, like gravitation and atmospheric pressure. Ruth Lannithorne is a good girl, I don't doubt. This world is chuck full of good girls. It makes some difference which one of 'em you marry, but not nearly so much difference as you think it does. What matters, from forty on, for the rest of your life, is the kind of inheritance you've given your children. You don't know it yet, but the thing that's laid on men and women to do is to give their children as good an inheritance as they can. Take it from me that this is gospel truth, can't you? Your mother and I have done the best we can for you and your sisters. You come from good stock, and by that I mean honest blood. You've got to pass it on untainted. Now--hold on!" he held up a warning hand as Oliver was about to interrupt hotly. "Wait till I'm through--and then think it over. I'm not saying that Peter Lannithorne's blood is n't as good as much that passes for untainted, or that Ruth isn't a fine girl. I'm only telling you this: when first you look into your son's face, every failing of your own will rise up to haunt you because you will wish for nothing on God's earth so much as that that boy shall have a fair show in life and be a better man than you. You will thank Heaven for every good thing you know of in your blood and in your wife's, and you will regret every meanness, every weakness, that he may inherit, more than you knew it was in you to regret anything. Do you suppose when that hour comes to you that you'll want to remember his grandfather was a convict? How will you face that down?"

Young Oliver's face was pale. He had never thought of things like this. He made no response for a while. At last he asked,--

"What kind of a man is Peter Lannithorne?"

"Eh? What kind of--? Oh, well, as men go, there have been worse ones. You know how he came to get sent up. He speculated, and he borrowed some of another man's money without asking, for twenty-four hours, to protect his speculation. He didn't lose it, either! There's a point where his case differs from most. He pulled the thing off and made enough to keep his family going in decent comfort, and he paid the other money back; but they concluded to make an example of him, so they sent him up. It was just, yes, and he said so himself. At the same time there are a great many more dishonest men out of prison than Peter Lannithorne, though he is in it. I meet 'em every day, and I ought to know. But that's not the point. As you said yourself, you don't want to marry their daughters. Heaven forbid that you should! You want to marry his daughter. And he was weak. He was tempted and fell, and got found out. He is a convict, and the taint sticks. The Lord knows why the stain of unsuccessful dishonesty should stick longer than the stain of successful dishonesty. I don't. But we know it does. That is the way things are. Why not marry where there is no taint?"

"Father--?"

"Yes, Ollie."

"Father, see here. He was weak and gave way--**once**! Are there any men in the world who have n't given way at least **once** about something or other?-- are there, father?"

There was a note of anguish in the boy's voice. Perhaps he was being pushed too far. Oliver Pickersgill Senior cleared his throat, paused, and at last answered somberly,--

"God knows, Ollie. I don't. I won't say there are."

"Well, then--"

"See here!" his father interrupted sharply. "Of course I see your argument. I won't meet it. I shan't try. It doesn't change my mind even if it is a good argument. We'll never get anywhere, arguing along those lines. I'll propose something else. Suppose you go ask Peter Lannithorne whether you shall marry his daughter or not. Yes, ask him. He knows what's what as well as the next man. Ask Peter Lannithorne what a man wants in the family of the woman he marries."

There was a note of finality in the older man's voice. Ollie recognized it drearily. All roads led to Lannithorne, it seemed. He rose, oppressed with the sense that henceforward life was going to be full of unforeseen problems; that things which, from afar, looked simple, and easy, and happy, were going to prove quite otherwise. Mrs. Lannithorne had angered rather than frightened him, and he had held his own with her, but this was his very own father who was piling the load on his shoulders and filling his heart with terror of the future. What was it, after all, this adventure of the married life whereof these seasoned travelers spoke so dubiously? Could it really be that it was not the divine thing it seemed when he and Ruth looked into each other s eyes?

He crossed the floor dejectedly, with the step of an older man, but at the door he shook himself and looked back.

"Say, dad!"

"Yes, Ollie."

"Everybody is so terribly depressing about this thing, it almost scares me. Aren't there really any happy times for married people, ever? You and Mrs. Lannithorne make me feel there are n't; but somehow I have a hunch that Ruth and I know best! Own up now! Are you and mother miserable? You never looked it!"

His father surveyed him with an expression too wistful to be complacent. Ah, those broad young shoulders that must be fitted to the yoke! Yet for what other end was their strength given them? Each man must take his turn.

"It's not a soft snap. I don't know anything worth while that is. But there are compensations. You'll see what some of them are when your boys begin to grow up."

IV

Across Oliver's young joy fell the shadow of fear. If, as his heart told him, there was nothing to be afraid of, why were his elders thus cautious and terrified? He felt himself affected by their alarms all the more potently because his understanding of them was vague. He groped his way in fog. How much ought he to be influenced by Mrs. Lannithorne's passionate protests and his father's stern warnings? He realized all at once that the admonitory attitude of age to youth is rooted deep in immortal necessity. Like most lads, he had never thought of it before save as an unpleasant parental habit. But fear changes the point of view, and Oliver had begun to be afraid.

Then again, before him loomed the prospect of his interview with Peter Lannithorne. This was a very concrete unpleasantness. Hang it all! Ruth was worth any amount of trouble, but still it was a tough thing to have to go down to the state capital and seek one's future father-in-law in his present boarding-place! One oughtn't to have to plough through that particular kind of difficulty on such an errand. Dimly he felt that the path to the Most Beautiful should be rose-lined and soft to the feet of the approaching bridegroom. But, apparently, that was n't the way such paths were laid out. He resented this bitterly, but he set his jaws and proceeded to make his arrangements.

It was not difficult to compass the necessary interview. He knew a man who knew the warden intimately. It was quickly arranged that he was to see Peter Lannithorne in the prison library, quite by himself.

Oliver dragged himself to that conference by the sheer strength of his developing will. Every fibre of his being seemed to protest and hold back. Consequently he was not in the happiest imaginable temper for important conversation.

The prison library was a long, narrow room, with bookcases to the ceiling on one side and windows to the ceiling on the other. There were red geraniums on brackets up the sides of the windows, and a canary's cage on a hook gave the place a false air of domesticity, contradicted by the barred sash. Beneath, there was a window-seat, and here Oliver Pickersgill awaited Lannithorne's coming.

Ollie did not know what he expected the man to be like, but his irritated nerves were prepared to resent and dislike him, whatever he might prove.

He held himself rigidly as he waited, and he could feel the muscles of his face setting themselves into hard lines.

When the door opened and some one approached him, he rose stiffly and held out his hand like an automaton.

"How do you do, Mr. Lannithorne? I am Oliver Pickersgill, and I have come--I have come--"

His voice trailed off into silence, for he had raised his eyes perfunctorily to Peter Lannithorne's face, and the things printed there made him forget himself and the speech he had prepared.

He saw a massive head topping an insignificant figure. A fair man was Peter Lannithorne, with heavy reddish hair, a bulging forehead, and deep-set gray eyes with a light behind them. His features were irregular and unnoticeable, but the sum-total of them gave the impression of force. It was a strong face, yet you could see that it had once been a weak one. It was a tremendously human face, a face like a battle ground, scarred and seamed and lined with the stress of invisible conflicts. There was so much of struggle and thought set forth in it that one involuntarily averted one's gaze. It did not seem decent to inspect so much of the soul of a man as was shown in Peter Lannithorne's countenance. Not a triumphant face at all, and yet there was peace in it. Somehow, the man had achieved something, arrived somewhere, and the record of the journey was piteous and terrible. Yet it drew the eyes in awe as much as in wonder, and in pity not at all!

These things were startlingly clear to Oliver. He saw them with a vividness not to be overestimated. This was a prison. This might be a convict, but he was a man. He was a man who knew things and would share his knowledge. His wisdom was as patent as his suffering, and both stirred young Oliver's heart to its depths. His pride, his irritation, his rigidity vanished in a flash. His fears were in abeyance. Only his wonder and his will to learn were left.

Lannithorne did not take the offered hand, yet did not seem to ignore it. He came forward quietly and sat down on the window-seat, half turning so that he and Oliver faced each other.

"Oliver Pickersgill?" he said. "Then you are Oliver Pickersgill's son."

"Yes, Mr. Lannithorne. My father sent me here--my father, and Mrs. Lannithorne, and Ruth."

At his daughter's name a light leaped into Peter Lannithorne's eyes that made him look even more acutely and painfully alive than before.

"And what have you to do with Ruth, or her mother?" the man asked.

Here it was! The great moment was facing him. Oliver caught his breath, then went straight to the point.

"I want to marry your daughter, Mr. Lannithorne. We love each other very much. But--I have n't quite persuaded her, and I have n't persuaded Mrs. Lannithorne and my father at all. They don't see it. They say things--all sorts of dreadful things," said the boy. "You would think they had never been young and--cared for anybody. They seem to have forgotten what it means. They try to make us afraid-- just plain afraid. How am I to suppose that they know best about Ruth and me?"

Lannithorne looked across at the young man long and fixedly. Then a great kindliness came into his beaten face, and a great comprehension. Oliver, meeting his eyes, had a sudden sense of shelter, and felt his haunting fears allayed. It was absurd and incredible, but this man made him feel comfortable, yes, and eager to talk things over.

"They all said you would know. They sent me to you."

Peter Lannithorne smiled faintly to himself. He had not left his sense of humor behind him in the outside world.

"They sent you to me, did they, boy? And what did they tell you to ask me? They had different motives, I take it."

"Rather! Ruth said you were the best man she had ever known, and if you said it was right for her to marry me, she would. Mrs. Lannithorne said I should ask you if you thought Ruth had a fighting chance for happiness with me. She does n't want Ruth to marry anybody, you see. My father--my father"--Oliver's voice shook with his consciousness of the cruelty of what was to follow, but he forced himself to steadiness and got the words out "said I was to ask you what a man wants in the family of the woman he marries. He said you knew what was what, and I should ask you what to do."

Lannithorne's face was very grave, and his troubled gaze sought the floor. Oliver, convicted of brutality and conscience-smitten, hurried on, "And now that I've seen you, I want to ask you a few things for myself, Mr. Lannithorne. I--I believe you know."

The man looked up and held up an arresting hand. "Let me clear the way for you a little," he said. "It was a hard thing for you to come and seek me out in this place. I like your coming. Most young men would have refused, or came in a different spirit. I want you to understand that if in Ruth's eyes, and my wife's, and your father's, my counsel has value, it is because they think I see things as they are. And that means, first of all, that I know myself for a man who committed a crime, and is paying the penalty. I am satisfied to be paying it. As I see justice, it is just. So, if I seem to wince at your necessary allusions to it, that is part of the price. I don't want you to feel that you are blundering or hurting me more than is necessary. You have got to lay the thing before me as it is."

Something in the words, in the dry, patient manner, in the endurance of the man's face, touched Oliver to the quick and made him feel all manner of new things: such as a sense of the moral poise of the universe, acquiescence in its retributions, and a curious pride, akin to Ruth's own, in a man who could meet him after this fashion, in this place.

"Thank you, Mr. Lannithorne," he said. "You see, it's this way, sir. Mrs. Lannithorne says--"

And he went on eagerly to set forth his new problems as they had been stated to him.

"Well, there you have it," he concluded at last. "For myself, the things they said opened chasms and abysses. Mrs. Lannithorne seemed to think I would hurt Ruth. My father seemed to think Ruth would hurt me. Is married life something to be afraid of? When I look at Ruth, I am sure everything is all right. It may be miserable for other people, but how could it be miserable for Ruth and me?"

Peter Lannithorne looked at the young man long and thoughtfully again before he answered. Oliver felt himself measured and estimated, but not found wanting. When the man spoke, it was slowly and with difficulty, as if the habit of intimate, convincing speech had been so long disused that the effort was painful. The sentences seemed wrung out of him, one by one.

"They have n't the point of view," he said. "It is life that is the great adventure. Not love, not marriage, not business. They are just chapters in the book. The main thing is to take the road fearlessly, to have courage to live one's life."

"Courage?"

Lannithorne nodded.

"That is the great word. Don't you see what ails your father's point of view, and my wife's? One wants absolute security in one way for Ruth; the other wants absolute security in another way for you. And security--why, it's just the one thing a human being can't have, the thing that's the damnation of him if he gets it! The reason it is so hard for a rich man to enter the kingdom of heaven is that he has that false sense of security. To demand it just disintegrates a man. I don't know why. It does."

Oliver shook his head uncertainly.

"I don't quite follow, sir. Ought n't one to try to be safe?"

"One ought to try, yes. That is common prudence. But the point is that, whatever you do or get, you are n't after all secure. There is no such condition, and the harder you demand it, the more risk you run. So it is up to a man to take all reasonable precautions about his money, or his happiness, or his life, and trust the rest. What every man in the world is looking for is the sense of having the mastery over life. But I tell you, boy, there is only one thing that really gives it!"

"And that is--?"

Lannithorne hesitated perceptibly. For the thing he was about to tell this undisciplined lad was his most precious possession; it was the piece of wisdom for which he had paid with the years of his life. No man parts lightly with such knowledge.

"It comes," he said, with an effort, "with the knowledge of our power to endure. That's it. ***You are safe only when you can stand everything that can happen to you.*** Then and then only! Endurance is the measure of a man."

Oliver's heart swelled within him as he listened, and his face shone, for these words found his young soul where it lived. The chasms and abysses in his path suddenly vanished, and the road lay clear again, winding uphill, winding down, but always lit for Ruth and him by the light in each other's eyes. For surely neither Ruth nor he could ever fail in courage!

"Sometimes I think it is harder to endure what we deserve, like me," said Lannithorne, "than what we don't. I was afraid, you see, afraid for my wife and all of them. Anyhow, take my word for it. Courage is security. There is no other kind."

"Then--Ruth and I--"

"Ruth is the core of my heart!" said Lannithorne thickly. "I would rather die than have her suffer more than she must. But she must take her chances like the rest. It is the law of things. If you know yourself fit for her, and feel reasonably sure you can take care of her, you have a right to trust the future. Myself, I believe there is Some One to trust it to. As for the next generation, God and the mothers look after that! You may tell your father so from me. And you may tell my wife I think there is the stuff of a man in you. And Ruth--tell Ruth--"

He could not finish. Oliver reached out and found his hand and wrung it hard.

"I'll tell her, sir, that I feel about her father as she does! And that he approves of our venture. And I'll tell myself, always, what you've just told me. Why, it *must* be true! You need n't be afraid I'll forget--when the time comes for remembering."

Finding his way out of the prison yard a few minutes later, Oliver looked, unseeing, at the high walls that soared against the blue spring sky. He could not realize them, there was such a sense of light, air, space, in his spirit.

Apparently, he was just where he had been an hour before, with all his battles still to fight, but really he knew they were already won, for his weapon had been forged and put in his hand. He left his boyhood behind him as he passed that stern threshold, for the last hour had made a man of him, and a prisoner had given him the master-key that opens every door.

THE LONG INHERITANCE

I

My niece, Desire Withacre, wished to divorce her husband, Dr. Arnold Ackroyd,--the young Dr. Arnold, you understand,--to the end that she might marry a more interesting man.

Other men than I have noticed that in these latter days we really do not behave any better than other people when it comes to certain serious issues of life, notably the marital. "We" means to me people of an heredity and a training like my own,--Americans of the old stock, with a normal Christian upbringing, who presumably inherit from their forebears a reasonable susceptibility to high ideals of living. I grew up with the impression that such a birth and rearing were a kind of moral insurance against the grosser human blunders and errors. Without vanity, I certainly did

"Thank the goodness and the grace
That on my birth had smiled."

It puzzled me for a long while, the light-hearted, careless way in which some of the younger Withacres, Greenings, Raynies, Fordhams, and so on (I name them out of many, because they are all kin to me) kicked over the traces of their family responsibilities. I could understand it in others but not in them.

It was little Desire Withacre who finally illuminated the problem for me. I am about to tell what I know of Desire's fling. If it seems to be a story with an undue amount of moral, I must refer the responsibility of that to Providence. The tale is of its making, not of mine.

I am afraid that, to get it all clearly before you, I shall have to prose for a while about the families involved.

I am Benjamin Stubbins Raynie, Desire's bachelor uncle, and almost the last of the big-nosed Raynies. My elder sister, Lucretia Stubbins Raynie, married Robert Withacre, one of the "wild Withacres" in whose blood there is a streak of genius and its revolts. The Withacres all have talent--mostly ineffectual--and keen aesthetic sensibilities. All of them can talk like angels from Heaven. By no stretch of the imagination can they be called thrifty. We considered it a very poor match for Lucretia. The Raynies are quiet people, not showy, but substantial and sensible; with a certain sentimental streak out-cropping here and there, especially in the big-nosed branch; while the red-headed Raynies are the better money-makers.

I know now that Lucretia secretly believed her offspring were destined to unite Withacre talent and Raynie poise. She prayed in her heart that the world might be the richer by a man child of her race who should be both gifted and sane. But her children proved to be twin girls, Judith and Desire. Queer little codgers I thought them, big-eyed, curly-headed, subdued when on exhibition. Lucretia told long stories, to which I gave slight attention, intended to prove that Judith was a marvelous example of old-head-on-young-shoulders, and that Desire, demure, elfin Desire, was a miracle of cleverness and winning ways.

In view of Desire's career, I judge that these maternal prepossessions were not wholly misplaced. As a small child she captivated her Uncle Greening as well as her aunt (our sister, Mary Stubbins Raynie, married Adam Greening of the well-known banking firm of Greening, Bowers & Co.). The Greenings were childless, and Desire spent much of her early life and nearly all her girlhood under Mary Greening's care and chaperonage. I confess to fondness for a bit of repartee with Desire now and then, myself. Perhaps I had my share in spoiling her. I take it a human being is spoiled when he grows up believing himself practically incapable of wrong-doing. That is what happened to Desire. Approval had followed her all of her days. How should she know, poor, petted little scrap, any thing about the predestined pitfalls of all flesh?

Of course the Robert Withacres were always as poor as poverty, and of course our family was always planning for and assisting them. Fortunately both the twins married early, and exceptionally well. Judith became engaged to a promising young civil engineer when visiting a school friend in Chicago. He said she reminded him of the New London girls. He was homesick, I think. At all events the engagement was speedy.

But our little Desire did better than that. She witched the heart out of young Arnold Ackroyd.

Do I need to explain the Ackroyds to any one? They are one of those exceptional families whose moral worth is so prominent that it even dims the lustre of their intellectual stability and their financial rating. They are so many other, better things that no one ever thinks or speaks of them as "rich." And in this day and generation that is real achievement.

Desire's marriage gratified me deeply, and for a wedding present I gave her the Queen Anne silver tea-set I inherited from great-aunt Abby. I believe in the Ackroyds, root and branch. They have, somehow or other, accomplished what all the rest of us are striving for. They have actually lifted an entire family connection to a plane where ability, worth, accomplishment, are matters of course. Nobody has ever heard of a useless, incompetent Ackroyd. Their consequent social preeminence, which possibly meant something to Mary Greening and which certainly counted with Desire, is merely incidental to their substantial merit. They are prominent for the rare reason that they deserve to be. They are the Real Thing.

Unless you happen to be in touch with them intellectually, however, this is not saying that you will always find all of them the liveliest of companions. The name connotes honor, ability, character; it does not necessarily imply humor, high spirits, the joy of life.

Desire herself told me of her engagement. I don't, somehow, forget how she looked when she came to tell me about it--shy, excited, radiant. She fluttered into my office and stood at the end of my desk, looking down at me. Desire was very pretty at twenty-one, with her pointed face and big expressive eyes, her white forehead shadowed by a heap of cloudy, curling, dark hair. Palpitating with life, she looked like some kind of a marvelous human hummingbird. It did not surprise me that Arnold Ackroyd found her

"All a wonder and a wild desire."

For all her excitement she spoke very softly.

"Uncle Ben, mother wants me to tell you something. I have n't told anybody else but her."

"What is it, Desire?"

"I--why, Uncle Ben--I've promised to marry Arnold Ackroyd!"

"Well, well," I said inadequately, "this is news!"

Desire nodded wistfully.

"It seems a little curious, does n't it? We're not a bit alike," she said. "But he is splendid! I'm sure I shall never meet a finer man, nor one I trust more."

"Very true, Desire, and I am glad you are going to marry such a man," I observed, arising slowly to the occasion and to my feet, and offering a congratulatory hand.

"Mother says it's a wonderful thought for a young woman that her future is as secure as the cycle of the seasons," returned Desire, with her hand in mine, "and I suppose it is, but that is n't why I love him. Uncle Ben, he's really wonderful when you find out what he's thinking behind those quiet eyes. And then--do you know he's one of the few really meritorious persons I ever made like me. I've been afraid there was something queer about me, for freaks always take to me at once. But if Arnold Ackroyd likes me, I *must* be all right, mustn't I? It's such a relief to be sure of it!"

I took this for a touch of flippancy, having forgotten how long the young must grope and wonder, hopelessly, before they find and realize themselves. It was, I think, precisely because Arnold Ackroyd helped that vibrant temperament to feel itself resting on solid ground that he became so easily paramount in Desire's life at this time. However it may have been afterward, during their brief engagement he was all things to my niece, while she to him was a creature of enchantment. I shall always maintain that they knew young love at its best.

Desire was wedded with more pomp and circumstance than Lucretia and I really cared for. That was her Aunt Greening's affair. Mary Greening always did like an effect of pageantry, and was willing to pay for it. They went abroad afterwards, and I remember as significant that Desire enjoyed the Musée de Cluny more than the lectures they heard at the Sorbonne. On their return they lived in dignity and comfort. They had a couple of pretty, unusual-looking children, who were provided with a French nurse at twenty months, and other educational conveniences in due season, more in accordance with the standards of Grandmamma Ackroyd than with the demands of the Withacres and Raynies.

They were certainly as happy as most people. If Desire had any ungratified wishes, I never heard of them. I dined with them frequently, but now see that I knew absolutely nothing about them. I took it for granted that they would always walk, as they seemed to be doing, in ways of pleasantness and peace.

It never entered my head that anybody of my own blood and a decent bringing-up could do what Desire did presently. I had a simple-minded notion that we were above it. Which brings me back to my premise. After all, we of a long inheritance of upright living do not always behave better than other people.

II

Lucretia was first to come.

The winter it all happened, I was house-bound with rheumatism and had no active part in the drama. By day I was wheeled into the little upstairs study and sat with my mind on chloroform liniment and flannels, while my family and friends came to me, bearing gifts. Sometimes they sought the house to amuse me, sometimes to relieve their minds.

Lucretia's burden was heaviest, so she was first.

The November morning was raw and hideous. There were flakes of snow on my sister's venerable and shabby sealskin. She laid back the veil on the edge of her little black bonnet,--she had been a widow for two years,-- brushed the snow from her slightly worn shopping-bag and sat down in front of the fire, pulling nervously at her gloves.

Lucretia is thin, sharp-featured ivory-skinned. Her aspect is both fatigued and ardent. Nothing that Mary and I were ever able to do for her lifted in the least from her own spirit the weight of her poverty-stricken, troublous, married life; and in her outer woman she persists in retaining that aspect of carefully brushed, valiantly borne adversity which is so trying to more prosperous and would-be-helpful kin.

I made a few comments on the weather, which Lucretia did not answer. Realizing suddenly that she was agitated, I became silent, hoping that the quiet, comfortable room, the snapping fire, and my own inertness, would act as a sedative. It did not occur to me that any really serious matter could be afoot. I had ceased to expect that life would offer any of us anything worse than occasional physical discomfort.

Having regained her composure, my sister spoke without preface.

"I am in great trouble, Benjamin. Desire has made up her mind to leave her husband, and nothing I say has the slightest effect."

"Good Heavens! Lucretia! What do you mean?"

"Just what I say. Desire declares she isn't satisfied as Arnold Ackroyd's wife. So she proposes to put an end to the relation. I judge she intends, later, to contract another marriage, though she is n't disposed to lay stress on that point."

I continued to look at Lucretia wide-eyed, and possibly wide-mouthed. The things she was saying were so preposterous, so incredible, that I could not accept them. It was as if I had received a message that the full moon was not "satisfied" to climb the evening sky.

"Lord! Lord! Little Desire!" I muttered.

"She is a woman of thirty, Benjamin."

"What does she say?" I exploded. "What is wrong in her married life? People don't do these things causelessly--not the people we are or know."

"She says a great deal," returned her mother dryly. "Did you ever know a Withacre to be lacking in words, Benjamin? Desire is very fluent. I might say she is eloquent."

"But what does it all amount to, anyhow?" I demanded impatiently. Dazed though I was, my consciousness of being the head of the family was returning.

Lucretia lifted her left hand, which was trembling, and checked off the items on her fingers. Her hands were shapely, though dark and shrunken, with swollen veins across the back. The firelight struck the worn gold of her wedding ring.

"She demands a less hampered life; a more variegated self-expression; a chance to help the world in her own way; an existence that shall be a daily development; the opportunity to give perpetual stimulus and refreshment to an utterly congenial mate. Oh! I know her reasons by heart," said Lucretia. "They sound like fine things, don't they, Benjamin?"

"Who is the other man?"

"Fortunately, none of us know him. He is a Westerner with one of those absurdly swollen fortunes. Desire would n't have thought it a wider life to marry a poorer man. Such women don't."

"I wish you would n't put Desire in a class and call her such women, Lucretia," I protested irritably.

My sister looked at me strangely.

"You, too? Can money buy you too?" she said.

She rose and steadied her trembling arms upon the low mantle. She stood, a black-clad figure, between me and the glowing hearth, looking down into the heart of the fire as she spoke. I had begun to perceive, vaguely, that here was no sister I had ever known before. In a way she was beside, or rather beyond, herself.

We Raynies are self-controlled people. Lucretia had always been a silent woman, keeping her emotions to her self. But they say earthquakes, vast convulsion of regions beneath the lowest seas, will sometimes force up to light of day strange flotsam from the ocean-bed. Things that the eyes of men have never seen, nor their busy minds conceived, float up to face the sun. From Lucretia's shaken soul arose such un-imagined things.

Her words came forth swiftly, almost with violence.

"Benjamin, my daughter proposes leaving for Reno, Nevada, next week to procure a divorce.--I'm not saying that plenty of divorces are n't justified. I know they are. Plenty of remarriages too, I make no doubt. I've lived long enough to know that extremes are always wrong, and the middle course is almost always right. I will admit, if you like, that every case is a thing apart, and stands on its own merits, and that only God and a woman's conscience are the judges of what she should do. But Desire's case has no merits!

"I know Arnold, and I know Desire; he is a busy man and she is an indulged woman. She might have entered into his life and interests if she had chosen; the door was as much open as it can be between a man and a woman. I don't claim it is ever easy for them to see clearly into each other's worlds. But they do it, every day. Here is Arnold working himself to death, reducing fractures and removing appendixes, and trying to make the people who swarm to him into whole and healthy men and women. That's a good way to help the world if you do it with every ounce of conscience there is in you. Here is Desire, fiddling with art and literature and civics and economics, and wanting to uplift the masses with Scandinavian dramas and mediaeval art and woman suffrage. If she really wants to enrich life for others, and she says she does, why, in Heaven's name, does n't she hold up Arnold Ackroyd's hands? There is work that is worth while, and it would take more brains and ability than she owns to do it well! It is **her** work; she chose it; she dedicated herself to it. Now she repudiates it for a whim."

"How do you know it is just a whim, Lucretia?" I interrupted rather shame-facedly. "Mightn't it be--er--a very violent attachment?"

Lucretia shook her head.

"These women nowadays are simply crazy about themselves. Are self-centred people ever capable of great passions?"

I made no protest, for I had thought the same thing myself.

"When they have dethroned their God and repudiated their families, what is there left to worship and work for but themselves?" she demanded grimly. "Half the women I meet are as mad for incense to their vanity as the men are mad for money."

"Lucretia," I said with all the firmness I could muster, "I do not think you ought to allow yourself to take this thing in this way. It is regrettable enough without working yourself up to such a pitch of agony."

She looked into the fire as if she had not heard me, and went rapidly on:--

"Sixty years ago, such things were unheard-of; forty years ago, they were a disgrace; twenty years ago, they were questioned; to-day, they are accepted. And yet they say the world advances! With all my troubles, Benjamin, I am just learning why men call death gracious--and my daughter is my teacher. Desire is at the restless age. I have seen a good many women between thirty and forty try to wreck their lives and other people's. You see, the dew is gone from the flowers. They have come to the heat and burden of the day. And they don't like it."

"You mean," I said, laboriously trying to follow her glancing thought in my own fashion, "that they miss the drama of early romance, and resent the fact that it has been replaced by the larger drama of responsibility and action?"

"That is a fine, sonorous way of putting it," she said bitterly, "but there are more forcible ways."

She laughed unpleasantly. I could feel the cruel words trembling on her lips, but she checked herself.

"Oh, what is the use of talking," she cried, "or of casting stones at other women? It doesn't help me to bear Desire's falling away. Benjamin, I would have known how to forgive a child who had sinned. I don't know how to forgive one who has failed like this! Desire is throwing away a life, not because it is intolerable, not because it is hard, even; but just because it has ceased to be exciting and amusing enough. But it is **her** life that she throws away. She cannot make a new one that will be real and her very own. She says she has ceased to love. They always say that. But love comes and goes always. There is no such thing as perpetual joy. Love is the morning vision. We are meant to hide that vision in our hearts and serve it on our knees. Good women know this and do it. That is what it means to be a wife. The vision is the thing we cherish and live for to the end. Desire is no cheated woman. She had young love at its best; she has her children's faces. There is such a thing as perpetual peace; life gives it to the loyally married. She might have had that, too. But she throws it all away--for novelty, for new sensations. My daughter is a wanton!"

"Lucretia!"

The energy of my ejaculation, the sight of my surprise, brought my sister back to her normal self. She dropped into her chair again, looking wan and shocked at her own violence of expression.

"You see how it is," she said humbly. "I am not fit to trust myself to talk about it. I ought to apologize for my language, Benjamin,--but that is the way I feel."

I had regained somewhat of my poise and my authority.

"See here, Lucretia, if this thing is to be, you must n't be so bitter about it. Desire is your daughter. She belongs to us. She has always been a pretty good girl. We must n't be too hard on her now, even if she does n't conform to our ideas. Everybody must live their own lives, you know."

Lucretia threw back her head; her deep-set eyes were burning, and the color suffused her face again.

"No!" she said sharply. "That must they not. Decent people accept some of the conclusions of their forebears and build upon the sure foundation reared by the convictions of their own people. You say she belongs to us. That is the worst of it! You childless man! Can't you guess what it would mean to bear, to nourish, to train,--to endure and endure, to love and love,--and then to have the flesh of your flesh turn on you and trample on all your sacredest things? It is the ultimate outrage. God knows whether I deserve it! God forgive me if I do!"

There was silence in the room. I had nothing more to say. I recognized at last how far Lucretia in her lonely agony was beyond any trite placation of mine.

After what seemed an age, she spoke. She was herself again. The violently parted waves had closed over the life of those far gray depths, and she offered her accustomed surface to my observation.

"I did not sleep at all last night, Benjamin. Desire was with me during the afternoon and we talked this thing out. I ought not to have seen any one so soon, but I came here with the intention of asking you to reason with her. I see it would do no good if you did. Things are as they are, and I must accept them. I will go home now. I am better off there."

She rose, put down her veil, drew on her gloves, and picked up the shabby shopping-bag, quietly putting aside my hesitating protestations and suggestions of luncheon.

At the door she turned and proffered a last word of extenuation for herself. "You ought to understand, for it is our blood in me that rebels. I never thought when I married a Withacre that I might bring into the world a child that wasn't *dependable*--but I might have known!" she said.

III

Lucretia, departing, left me tremulous. The flame-like rush of her mind had scorched my consciousness; the great waves of her emotion had pounded and beaten me. I shared, and yet shrank from, her passionate apprehension of our little Desire's failure in the righteous life. For I was, and am, fond of Desire.

I spent a feverish and most miserable day. There were so many unhappy things to consider! The gossip that would rack the town apparently did not concern Lucretia at all. I am hide-bound, I dare say, and choked with convention. Certainly I shrank from the notoriety that would attach itself to us when young Mrs. Arnold Ackroyd took up her residence in Reno, as a first step toward the wider life. Then there was the disruption of old ties of friendship and esteem. It would be painful to lose the Ackroyds from among our intimates, yet impossible to retain them on the old footing. I already had that curious feeling of having done the united clan vicarious injury.

Toward five o'clock my sister Mary, Mrs. Greening, tapped on the door.

Mary Greening and I are good friends for brother and sister. As children we were chums; we abbreviated for each other the middle name we all bore, Mary calling me Stub, and I calling her Stubby. We meant this to express exceptional fraternal fealty. It was like a mystic rite that bound us together.

She came in almost breezily. For a woman in late middle life Mary Greening is comely. There is at the bottom of her nature an indomitable youthfulness, to which her complexion and movements bear happy witness.

"Well, Stub, has Lucretia been here?"

"Come and sit down, Mary. Yes, Lucretia has been here. Very much so," I answered dejectedly.

Mary swept across the room almost majestically. Quite the type of a fine woman is Mary Greening, though perhaps a thought too plump. She threw back her sable stole and unfastened her braided violet coat; she prefers richly embellished garments, though they are thought garish by some of the matrons in her set.

"You keep it much too warm in here," she said critically.

I made a grimace.

"Your hat is a little to one side, Stubby, as usual."

She put her hand up tentatively to the confection of fur, yellow lace, and violet orchids.

"I don't think Lenore ballasts my hats properly," she said plaintively. "It can't be my fault that they slide about so. But I did n't come to talk about hats."

I sighed. "No, you came to talk about Desire. Mary, how long have you known about this deplorable affair?"

"Oh--ever since there has been anything to know! Desire has always talked to me more than to her mother. You know, Ben, one would n't choose Lucretia as a confidante in any kind of a heart affair."

"Don't put on that worldly air with me, Mary Greening," I said crossly. "Lucretia is a little austere, but it seems to me that austerity has its advantages. For instance, it keeps one out of the newspapers. Am I to infer that you sympathize with Desire?"

"Not at all," she protested. "You may not believe me, but I have suffered and suffered, over this thing. I can't count the nights I have lain awake thinking about it. At first it seemed to me I simply could not have it, and I thought I was going to influence Desire. But nobody ever influences people in matters of the heart. Of course this is an affair on the highest possible plane--so I thought they might be more reasonable. But I don't observe that they are."

"On the highest possible plane," I mused. "Mary, be candid with me. I would like a good woman's point of view on this. If a game of hearts ends in the courts, breaking up a home and smashing the lives concerned to flinders, do you really think it matters whether that affair is on a high plane or a low one? Does it seem any better to you for being the finer variety?"

"Certainly it does," returned Mary Greening promptly; "though," she added reflectively, "judged by results, I see it is illogical to feel so."

She cogitated a little longer.

"You put the thing too crudely. Here is the point, Ben. The Devil never makes the mistake of offering the coarser temptation to persons of taste. You couldn't have tempted Desire to break up her home with any temptation that did n't include her intellect, her spirit, and her aesthetic instincts. And when one gets up in that corner of one's nature, people like you or me or Desire are so used to regarding all the demands emanating from there as legitimate, as something to be proud of, to be satisfied at almost any cost, that it takes a very clear sense of right and wrong to prevent confusion. And, nowadays, hardly anybody but old fogies and back numbers, and people who have lived the kind of life Lucretia has, possesses a clear sense of right and wrong. It has gone out."

"What became of Desire's married happiness, Mary? I thought there was so much of it, and that it was of a durable variety."

"Oh, it leaked away through small cracks, as happiness usually does. It is hard to explain to a man, but if Arnold were a woman, you might almost say that he nagged. He is too detailed, too exact, for Desire. If, for instance, she said in May, I believe I will have a green cloth, embroidered, for a fall suit, about the first of November, you might expect Arnold to remark, I don't see that green cloth suit you said you were going to have. What made you change your mind? Desire delights to say things she does n't mean and lay plans she does n't expect to carry out, so a constant repetition of such incidents was really pretty wearing. I have seen her when she reminded me of a captive balloon in a high wind.

"A woman in your position ought not to make unconsidered speeches was one of his pet remarks. He is scientific, she is temperamental--and each of them expected the other one to be born again, and born different by virtue of mutual affection and requirements. Arnold will go on wondering to the end of his life why Desire can't be more accurate, more purposeful. As if he did n't fall in love with her the way she is! And then along comes the Westerner--"

"Where did they meet?"

"Bessie Fleming introduced them--at some silly place like Atlantic City. It was after Desire had that nervous breakdown two years ago. I know they were both in wheeled chairs at the time, and they rode up and down together, talking, like long-separated twin souls, about the theory of aesthetics and kindred matters. They did n't require diagrams to see each other's jokes, and that is always a strong tie. He was a man used to getting what he wanted, and when he became bewitched--can't you see how it would all work together? I know Lucretia thinks there is no excuse for Desire. But I see this excuse for her. None of us ever trained her to know she could n't have everything she wanted. Of course, we never expected her to want anything but the finest, the highest. But she is human, and when she found a most wonderful thing in her path that she wanted more than she had ever wanted anything before--she put out her hand to take it, as she had taken other things when we were all applauding her choice. And I will do her the justice to say that I don't believe she has the faintest notion Arnold will really fight to keep the children. You see, she still thinks the world is hers."

"Perhaps it is," I offered. The comfort of Mary's presence was beginning to rest and appease me, and I was a little less conscious of my aching conscience. "The Westerner--is he--is he--"

"Perfectly presentable. Quite a scholar. Collects pictures. Has all kinds of notions. He and Desire are ideally congenial. Very properly he is keeping himself at long distance and entirely out of it. No one but ourselves surmises that he exists. And it really is an enormous fortune. I can imagine Desire doing all kinds of interesting things with it."

"Do you know what Lucretia said to me, Mary?"

She shook her head.

"You, too? Can money buy you, too?" I quoted. "I shall never forget how Lucretia looked as she said it."

"Stub--the world moves. It may be moving in the wrong direction, but if we don't move with it, we are bound to be left behind."

"Mary Greening," I retorted, "do you really mean that you detect in yourself a willingness to have an unjustified divorce and a huge, vulgar fortune in the family, just because they are up to date?"

"Benjamin Raynie, if down at the bottom of my soul there is crawling and sneaking a microscopical acquiescence in the muddle Desire is making of life, it is probably due to the reason you mention. I am just as ashamed of it as I can be! I ought to be plunged in grief, like Lucretia. And I ***am***--only-- well, I want to help Desire, and I can't help her if I let myself feel like that. I suppose you'll think I'm an unmoral old thing, but I see it this way: if these affairs are going to happen in one's very own family, one might as well put them through with a high hand. I intend to stand by Desire. Of course the Ackroyds will do the same by Arnold. Desire will never be received in this town again with their consent. They are entirely in the right. But I shall have to fight them for Desire's sake, just the same."

"Stubby! Stubby! There is n't a particle of logic as big as a pin-head about you, and I don't approve of you at all--but I do like you tremendously!"

Mary Greening rose abruptly, crossed to the window, and stood looking out for a time. Then she came back and, dropping awkwardly beside my chair, buried her convulsed and quivering face in the woolly sleeve of my jacket, while the tears dripped fast from her overflowing eyes.

"Stub," she brought out jerkily, between her sudden choking sobs, "I did n't make a long face and tell Desire 'whom God hath joined'--I--I tried to appeal to her common sense. Irreligious people often do have a great deal of common sense, you know. But--I am the child of our fathers, too. I wish--I *wish* she would n't do it!"

IV

I certainly expected that Desire would come to me before she went away. I don't know what good I thought it would do. But we had always (or I supposed so) been such friends, this niece and I, that I could not believe she would take such an important step without an effort to gain my approval--my toleration would be more accurate. I--well, I thought she cared for my approval. But it seemed she did n't.

Of course, when one came to think it over, she could hardly enjoy such an interview. No doubt she was already sore in spirit from interviews she could not shirk,--with her mother, for instance, not to mention her husband. And my views on promiscuous divorce are as well known in the family as are those of South Carolina. They are simple, those views, and old-fashioned, but also, I may add, cosmic; they run about as follows: it is hard that John and Mary should be unhappy, but better their discomfort than that society should totter to a fall, since all civilization rests upon the single institution of the marriage tie. I will admit that my bachelor state doubtless helps to keep my opinions uncomplicated.

When I came to think of it in the light of these convictions, it was n't remarkable that Desire stayed away. And yet the foolish old uncle in me was hurt that she did so. I felt that she ought to come and take her medicine. Did n't thirty years of affection and indulgence give me some rights in her life?

Perhaps Mary Greening told her how I felt. At all events, in place of a call I received a letter:--

DEAR UNCLE BEN,--

The reason I'm not coming to say good-bye to you is that I think you'll love me better if I don't. My self-control is wearing quite thin in spots, and I'm so tired of explaining myself (when there's nothing to explain except that I am doing what seems right in my own eyes) that sometimes I think I shall just die before I get started.

Uncle Ben, did n't you ever long for a life that fitted you exactly,-- a life that was the flexible, soft garment of your very Self? I am laying aside a life that is somewhat cumbrous for me, and going to one that, fits me like a glove.

And it is n't as if my case were like other people's, or as if Arthur Markham was n't the finest of the fine. He is as good in his widely different way as Arnold is. I think myself a highly fortunate woman that two such lives are offered me to choose from--but I must choose the one that belongs to me. Temperament is destiny. I am following mine. I am doing what I wish to do. But I don't like the way people hinder me with arguments that have nothing to do with the real content of the matter. So I am saying good-bye at arm's length to the dearest old make-believe cynic of an uncle that ever lived. Because you know, Uncle Ben, that if you had me there you could n't help preaching to me, and I am tired of preaching. It does n't get one anywhere. And it does n't keep one away--from Reno, Nevada.

I suppose it's a queer thing to say but, really, you'll like Arthur just as well as you do Arnold--if only you can bring your mind to it!

I am always, even in Nevada,

Your loving niece,

DESIRE.

I turned this letter over curiously in my hands, half expecting it to impart to me the secret of how it was that people could think and feel as if the very universe wheeled, glittering, about them and their desires. Also, how could Desire be so guiltless of all the thousand scruples and delicacies that were her birthright? How could she exhibit such poverty of spirit, bravely and unashamed? How did it happen that she, of all people, showed herself so ignorant of the things that cannot be learned?

V

That evening as I drowsed over the hearth after dinner, still holding Desire's letter in my hand and pondering over it, the card of young Dr. Arnold Ackroyd was brought up to me.

I awoke myself with a start. An interview with Desire's husband was the last thing in the world I wanted. The feeling that I had vicariously injured the Ackroyds was still strong upon me, and I shrank childishly from facing a man whom I could not think of otherwise than as a maimed and wantonly injured creature.

Feeling this, I naturally welcomed him with a mixture of embarrassment and effusion. Dr. Arnold smiled dryly, with perfect comprehension, and took his seat beside the fire in the same winged armchair that had sheltered Lucretia and Mary previously. A fancy seized me that the cumbersome, comfortable piece of mahogany and old brocade might indeed be a veritable witness-seat, a Chair of Truth, that in some fashion impelled its occupant to speak out from the heart the thing he really thought. An apprehensive glance at Arnold's grave, clear-cut, sallow face reassured me. It held no threat of hysteric protest. Whatever he might say, I need not fear that he would break the inmost silence of a deeply humiliated man.

"It is a matter of business that I want to see you about, Mr. Raynie," he said easily. "There is no one but you who can manage it for me."

I expressed my desire to serve him.

"You see, it is just this: if Desire insists upon divorcing me the enterprise must be properly financed. I prefer to pay her expenses myself. I am not going to have her hard up or--depending upon any one else."

"Desire would never take money from any one but Mrs. Greening or me, Ackroyd."

"No--I suppose not. Still, you never can tell how these confounded modern women are going to invert things in their minds. She'd not do it unless she could make it look high-minded and self-sacrificing, of course. But I would rather she ran no risk of doing it. And, if you don't mind my saying so, I would also prefer at present that even you and Mrs. Greening kept your hands out of your pockets. You see, Desire is my wife until she ceases to be so. It is unquestionably my right to provide for her, even in Reno, if I choose. Of course, she would say that, having left my bed and board, she had renounced her claim upon my bank account--that is, she would say it if she thought about the matter at all. But she is so heedless she will probably not question the source of supplies, certainly not if they come through you. Will you do me this favor, Mr. Raynie?"

There was nothing for me to do but assent, but I did so a little irritably. It seemed to me at the moment that it would be excellent discipline to let the winds of heaven beat harshly upon Desire's delicately guarded head, for a short time at least. I intimated as much.

Arnold Ackroyd shook his head.

"It is too late for that kind of discipline to be effective," he said. "I have meant that Desire should have everything that a man can give, but there is one point I will never yield. She shall not have my children!"

He took out his checkbook and his pen, and, writing on his knee, filled out a check rapidly and neatly.

As he handed it to me I noted that the sum was surprisingly large,-- enough for a divorce *de luxe*. "Pardon me, but are n't you overdoing your generosity, Arnold?" I suggested.

He moved his shoulders very slightly, and I saw his fine, surgeon's fingers stir as though he were involuntarily washing his hands of the whole question of money.

"Desire is accustomed to beauty as well as to comfort," he said. Then he dropped his head on his chest and stared gravely into the fire. "Mr. Raynie, what do the women want? What do they expect in this world, anyhow? If the sun had dropped out of the sky, it wouldn't have surprised me more than this thing has."

"Nor me," I confessed.

"I have been wondering if I unconsciously neglected Desire? People say that sometimes causes them to fly the track. I am a busy man. I work hard in an exacting profession. But, as I understand the marriage contract, my work is a part of what I endowed her with. It is my life, myself. We are not children. One does not marry for a playmate, does one? But perhaps women do. Do you think I can have been at fault in this matter?"

My only answer was an impatient snort of protest.

"I supposed she desired companionship with me as I am. Certainly that was what I thought I asked of her. She has such a way of making life seem vivid and interesting that her companionship was good to have," he said.

Something clutched at my heart strings as I saw the look of inextinguishable longing in his eyes.

"We spoiled her between us, I suspect," he said. "On our heads be it, for it is spoiled that she is. Mr. Raynie, I think of Desire as undisciplined, wayward--not as wanton.--Well, I have a dozen patients yet to see to-night. I must say good night, and thank you."

As he closed the door, I spoke aloud to myself and the witness-chair.

"There goes a gentleman," I said. "It seems they still exist. Confound that niece of mine!"

VI

After Desire departed for Reno, the winter dragged along, heavy-footed.

Mary Greening heard from her often, and brought me the letters. She rented a cottage in Reno, and began housekeeping bravely, but, presently, the servant question drove her temporarily to a hotel.

Very shortly we saw in the papers an account of a fire in the same hotel. This was followed by a telegram from Desire to the effect that she was as right as possible, and had only suffered the loss of a few garments.

A week later as I sat in my usual place, the wheeled chair by the study fire, I heard a carriage stop at my door. It was ten o'clock of a wild January night, furious with wind and snow. There were voices in the hall below; surprised ejaculations from Lena, the housemaid; at last a rap on my door, which swung inward to admit--Desire!

"Will you take me in, Uncle Ben?" she inquired cheerfully. "It is such a frightful night! The cabman won't try to get me to Aunt Mary. He wanted to leave me at a hotel. But this was no farther--and I wanted to talk with you, anyhow."

I said the appropriate things, consumed meanwhile with wonder as to what this reappearance meant. Desire threw off her long wrap and her furs, vibrated about the room a little, then settled, like every one else, in the winged chair across the hearth, and smiled at me tremulously.

"Uncle Ben, something has happened to me."

"I judge it is something important, Desire."

"A big thing," she said gravely. "So big I don't understand it. I can only tell you how it is."

I waited quietly, but there was that in her voice which made me catch my breath.

She seemed to find it hard to begin.

"I hated Reno," she said at last, abruptly. "The streets were so full of plump, self-satisfied blonde women, overdressed and underbred. The town was overrun with types one did n't like. It was--horrid! But it did n't concern me, so I stayed in the little house and wrote a great many letters to Aunt Mary and--Arthur Markham, and read, and amused myself as best I could. Then I lost my maids and moved to the hotel until I could arrange matters.

"You heard about the fire? The hotel was a wooden building with two wings, and my room was in the wing that burned. It was all very exciting, but I got out with my valuables and most of my wardrobe tied up in a sheet, and they put the fire out.

"The rest of the building was unhurt, so the occupants opened their doors to the people who had been burned out. The manager asked me if I would accept the hospitality of a Mrs. Marshall, 'a very nice lady from up North!' I said I would be thankful for shelter of any description, so he took me to her door and introduced us."

Desire paused reflectively.

"I'd like to make it as clear as possible to you, Uncle Ben, if you don't mind my talking a lot. This Mrs. Marshall was just a girl, and very good-looking indeed in a way. She had well-cut features, a strong chin, blue eyes under dark lashes, and a great deal of vitality. So far as looks went, I might have met her anywhere.

"The big room was strewn with her things, for she had expected to be burned out, too; but she began to put them away at once, offering me closet room, and talking excitedly as she moved about.

"The place was full of department-store luxury, if you know what I mean. Her toilet-table was loaded with silver in a pattern of flamboyant, curly cupids,--I've often wondered who bought such things,--and there were gorgeous, gaudy garments lying about. Her belongings, all but a few frocks, were expensive and tasteless to the last degree. So much extravagance and so little beauty! It seemed so strange to me that it was interesting.

"She talked a good deal, showing me this and that. Her slangy speech had a certain piquancy, because she looked finer than her words. She was absolutely sure of herself, and at ease. I made out that this was because she was conscious of no standards save those of money, and there, as she would have said, she could 'deliver the goods.' Were n't the evidences of her worth right under my eyes?

"I talked, too, as effusively as I knew how. I tried to meet her halfway. She was evidently a perfectly well-placed and admired person in her own world. I was excited and tired and lonely. It seemed good just to speak to some one.

"Presently the room was cleared, and we began to think of sleeping. I have n't forgotten a word of the conversation that followed.

"'It's very good of you to take me in. I hope I shan't disturb you very much,' I said.

"'Oh, I'm glad to have somebody to talk to. I think this living in Reno is deadly, but it seems to be the easiest way to get results,' she answered. 'How long you been here?'

"I told her.

"'Well, I'm a good deal nearer my freedom than you are. Don't it seem perfectly ridiculous that when you want to shake a man you can't just **shake** him, without all this to-do?' she said. 'It makes me so mad to think I've got to stay down here six months by myself, just to get rid of Jim Marshall! Say, what does your husband do?'

"What could I say, Uncle Ben? It seemed sacrilegious to mention Arnold in that room, but I was her guest and dependent upon her for shelter and a bed.

"'He is a doctor,' I said.

"'That so? Jim's superintendent of a mine. Up in the mountains. It's the lonesomest place you ever saw. Twenty miles from nowhere, with just a little track running down to the rail road, and nothing worth mentioning when you get there.

"'Jim was awfully gone on me. Put up a spiel that he could n't live without me, and all that. That was two years ago, and I was young and tender hearted. Father had just dropped a whole bunch of money, and I thought, 'Well, if any man wants to pay my bills as bad as that, I guess I'll let him.' It looked like easy meal-tickets to me. Say! There.s no such thing as a soft snap in married life. You got to work for your living, whoever he is. And I got so bored up in the mountains I did n't know what to do. Any man's a bore if you see too much of him. Jim's awful soft--wants to be babied all the time. Thought I did n't love him unless I looked just so and talked just so. Jerusalem! How can you love anybody when you're a hundred miles from a matinee? People have got to have what they're used to, even if they are married, and that's a cinch. I used to go down to the city by myself once in a while to visit Jim's sister, but there was n't anything in that. She and I did n't get on. She never took me to a show once all the time I was there. These in-laws are always looking at you through a microscope. Ain't it awful? I don't claim my complexion will stand that scrutiny. Did you have any in-laws?'

"'A few,' I said, thinking how Madam Ackroyd would look if she could hear this conversation.

"'Well, anybody can have mine!' she said. 'Gee! How I hate to be bored! I guess I'd be up on that mountain yet if it hadn't been for that. Last spring the son of the man who owns the mine took to coming up to see about the output. I had him going in forty winks. I was just amusing myself, but Jim got frightfully jealous. "See here," I says, "I ain't going to let no mining man dictate to me, see? I'll tell you that right now!" I was sore. To think he could n't let me have a bit of fun, after the stupid winter I'd put in, frying his bacon. It seemed plain selfish. So things ran along, and I got huffier and huffier. Finally, when Joe volunteered he'd like to put up for me to take this trip to Reno, I packed my suit-case and came away. It served Jim right for being such an old grouch. What'd you think?'

"I just opened my mouth and gasped. I could n't help it. Such callousness!

"The girl looked at me queerly when I did n't answer. 'What's got *you* that you did n't stay put?' she demanded. 'Here I've had a rush of words to the mouth and told you all I know and I don't know a thing about you.'

"I found my voice sufficiently to tell her my case was very different.

"'Huh!' she said, 'I may n't know much, but I'm wise to this; the folks that have real reasons for a smash-up don't have to come to Reno. They mostly can get their papers on the spot. I guess we're all in the same boat out here. We're just taking what we want.'

"I felt as if I had been struck with a sledge-hammer when she said that, and her eyes seemed to be boring through me like gimlets. I thought I should scream if she said another word.

"'Let's talk about it in the morning,' I said, 'if you'll excuse me. I'm so tired I simply can't keep my eyes open.'

"That was n't true. She went to sleep almost instantly, and slept like a baby. I lay beside her, wide awake for hours. What she was, and what she said, had turned a key in my brain. A host of thoughts I didn't know I had came trooping out of some hidden room, and they marched and counter-marched across my mind all night."

Desire got up and began to walk about the room restlessly in her absorption as she recalled all this.

"It was wonderful, Uncle Ben. I wish I could make you understand. First of all, I recognized that what she said was absolutely true. I said to myself, Desire, you are a civilized, cultivated, mature, distinguished-looking person, well born and well reared--but what has it all done for you? It has, precisely, conducted you to Reno, Nevada. This girl beside you is uncivilized, uneducated, crude, young, clearly of very common clay. And what has it all done for her but conduct her to Reno, Nevada,--where she finds you, daughter of the Pilgrims. Well met, sister!'

"It was very bitter to think that of myself," said my niece, stopping by my chair. "It may sound foolish, Uncle Ben, but my friends have always insisted I was a ***schöne Seele***. I, a beautiful soul! I, a soul at all! A white light that I could not shut my eyes against seemed to beat down into my brain. I saw that I was just like the girl beside me in her incredible callousness,--even like the fat, self-satisfied, blonde women I had seen in the town. Oh, those common, common people! I had thought myself as fine as silk, as tempered as steel, yes, and as pure as flame! But I, too, was a brute.

"I thought and thought. I thought of Arnold, Arthur, and myself; we are all proud, we are all fastidious, yet we had come to this. We had drifted on the rocks. Pride had n't saved us, nor training, nor intelligence. I had lived in and for these things, and they had not prevented my doing the commonest things like the commonest creatures. Uncle Ben, I seemed horrible to myself--I can't tell you.

"More doors opened in my mind, and I began to think of you, and mother, and Aunt Mary, and of all the stories you used to tell me of the good Raynies and the bad, the weak Withacres and the strong ones, and what good fighters there were among them. And it seemed to me that I could see and feel--like the flight of wings in the dark over my head-- the passing of the struggling generations of my fathers, each one achieving a little more; going from decency to good repute, and from repute to renown, keeping faith with one another and with God, from father to son.

"And all at once I saw that the dignity of my race did not consist in its honors, nor even in its character, but--forever and always--in its fight for character! It was the struggle that had made us. And I had never struggled--so--I was not made. I was still unformed, shapeless,--and a cheaper thing with all my pretensions than the girl asleep beside me.

"Then there came on me a great desire to be one with my own people. One life is nothing--somehow I saw it very clearly. Families build righteousness as coral insects build a reef. I felt the yearning to be built into a structure of honesty and honor. Even as I wished this, I saw, in that fierce light beating down upon my brain, that there was something deep within me that forbade me to do the thing I had been planning. It lay at the core of being, dark and stern; it said ***No*** to my desires. And I knew it for the strength of every ***No*** my fathers ever uttered. It was my inheritance. And as I looked, it seized my will. It shook me free from my longing for Arthur, free from my impatience with Arnold, free from my wish to have my way!

"So--I have come back. It was strong enough to bring me back; it is strong enough to hold me here. I don't care what happens to me after this. ***I don't care.*** I may not be happy, but I don't seem to want to be happy: I want to do the seemly, fitting things, the decent things. I don't care if they are stupid; I don't care if I am bored! I wish just what I say. I want to be one with my race. It is they who have brought me back. They held up the torch. I let it fall. Uncle Ben, do you think it has gone out? Suppose one of my children's children should stumble and then say, 'It is not my fault. I inherited this. There was grandmamma who went her willful way so long ago!' I know my dust would shiver in the ground. I can't add any more to the weaknesses and follies that will crush them down. Having my own way costs too much when they must pay. That's it. I have n't the price. I refuse to let them pay.--Will you help me, Uncle Ben? Will you ask Arnold to let me try again? I will be good. I will be humble--almost! For I must have my children if only that I may pass this on. The thing is to abolish our complacency. Why--it's what the old religionists meant when they talked about getting down in the dust before their God! It really, really, is the thing we have to do. And-- my children will never learn it here, among you, where everybody is so happy and self-satisfied. They will never learn it even from the righteous Arnold. If they know it, they will have to learn it from me-- for I am the only repentant sinner of us all! So--I have come back."

Desire's words stirred me strangely. I had sometimes suspected that I allowed my modest pride of descent to feed complacency rather than effort. As she talked, I, too, saw the long procession of the valiant men and women of my race moving forward through the years; I saw how I had lightly arrogated credit to myself for their hard-won excellencies, and reckoned myself a finer gentleman for the battles they had fought. Where were my battles? Where my victories?

Then--I remembered that the Withacres always could talk like angels from heaven. But I looked into Desire's eyes, and that thought shriveled before the flame in them. They met mine exultantly, as steel meets steel. This was no lip eloquence. She was eager for her battles.

"So," I said with wonder, "you have capitulated--to Them."

"Yes--to Them. Oh, it is n't needful, Uncle Ben, that to show my kinship I should work as they did, live as plainly, think as narrowly. It is all here just the same. I am their child. I will not go against their will. Before ever I was born, they wrote their desires in my flesh. They made the blood to flow in my veins after their ways. And--I am glad! For my children shall be their children.--Uncle Ben, will Arnold take me home?"

I looked at Desire's glowing face that seemed afire with aspiration for the life she had tossed aside. I thought of Arnold's grave lips, steady shoulders, and longing eyes. There fell upon me a vivid sense of the wonderful ingenuity and richness of life's long processes. This diverse pair had traveled devious ways to the end that, after all their married years, they might at last be not unequally mated. My elderly heart sang a canticle of rejoicing, but my speech was circumspect.

"I incline to believe that he will," I admitted.

CLARISSA'S OWN CHILD

I

It was half-past three o'clock on a Tuesday afternoon in April when Associate Professor Charleroy (of the Midwest University at Powelton) learned that he was to lose his wife and home.

For April, the day was excessively hot. The mercury stood at eighty-nine degrees on the stuffy little east porch of the Charleroy home. There was no ice in the refrigerator, the house-cleaning was not finished, and the screens were not in. The discomfort of the untimely heat was very great.

Clarissa Charleroy, tired, busy, and flushed of face, knew that she was nervous to the point of hysteria. This condition always gave her a certain added clearness of vision and fluency of speech which her husband, with justice, had learned to dread. Indeed, she dreaded it herself. In such moods she often created for herself situations which she afterwards found irksome. She quite sincerely wished herself one of the women whom fatigue makes quiet and sodden, instead of unduly eloquent.

Paul Charleroy, coming from a classroom, found his wife in the dining-room, ironing a shirt-waist. The door was open into the little kitchen beyond, where the range fire was burning industriously, and the heat poured steadily in.

"I thought it would be cooler in here," Clarissa explained wearily, "but it is n't. I have to get these waists ready to wear, and a gingham dress ironed for Marvel. The child is simply roasted in that woolen thing. But the starch *will* stick to the irons!"

Professor Charleroy shut the door into the kitchen. He frowned at the ironing-board, balanced on two chairs in front of the window. Small changes in the household arrangements were likely to discompose him. In his own house he was vaguely conscious always of seeking a calm which did not exist there.

"Can't the washerwoman do that ironing?" he inquired.

Clarissa dropped her iron and confronted him dramatically.

"Doubtless--if I could afford to pay her," she responded. "As you are already aware, the salary of associate professors in the Midwest University is fourteen hundred dollars a year. When steak was a shilling a pound and eggs fifteen cents a dozen and the washerwoman asked a dollar a day, one could afford to have her help longer. Now it is different."

Professor Charleroy moved quietly over to the ironing-board and put the flatiron, which was still hot enough to scorch, upon its stand. Then he arranged, in a glass, the handful of daffodils he was carrying, and set them where the April sunshine fell across them.

"Yes, I know it is different," he said gloomily. "But it may be different again if I can place my text-book. When we married, Clarissa, I thought your own little income would be sufficient to protect you from such economies as I knew would be most distasteful to you--but, somehow, it--it does n't seem to do it."

"It goes," returned Clarissa. "I don't know how it goes, but it does. I dare say I'm not a good manager. It is n't as if I dressed well, for I don't. But I would n't mind, if we could go to Chicago for a week of music and theatres in the spring. But we can't do anything but live--and *that* is n't living! Something is wrong with the whole system of woman's work in the world. I don't know what it is, but I mean to find out. Somebody has got to do something about it."

She threw back her small blonde head as she spoke, and it was as if she gave the universe and all its powers warning that she did not purpose to live indefinitely under such an ill-arranged order of things as they were maintaining. Let the universe look to itself!

"I met Baumgarten of the Midwest Ice Company on the campus. He says if this weather holds, he will start his ice-wagons to-morrow," suggested her husband anxiously. He had very definite reasons for wishing to divert Clarissa from consideration of all the things that are out of joint in the world.

"Ice is a detail. Sometimes details do help," admitted Clarissa, fanning her blazing cheeks.

"We will have Jacob come and wash the windows and put on the screens in the morning," he continued very gently. "And I will uncover the roses and rake the beds this afternoon. I should have done it last week, but no one could forsee this weather."

"I'm not ready for Jacob until I have been through the closets. They must be cleaned first.--I hate to clean closets! I hate to cook, to sew, to iron, to dust, to scrub! There are women who like these occupations. Let such people assume them!"

"I can hear you, Clarissa, if you speak less oratorically. We are not in an audience-room," suggested her husband.

Clarissa was slender, fair, and dramatic. If she was in the room you looked at her. Her Norman nose was delicately cut, her manner fastidious, but her collars were carelessly put on, and her neckties had a vaguely one-sided effect. She just escaped being pretty and precise and reliable-looking by a narrow margin, but escape she did. She was, instead, disturbing, distracting, decidedly lovable, not a little pathetic. Her face was dreamy, yet acute--the face of an enthusiast. The line of her jaw was firmly and beautifully drawn; her intellectual activity was undeniable, but philistines mistrusted her conclusions at sight--and justly.

"This is not a good day on which to hold an argument," she went on with dignity, ignoring her husband's sub-acid comment. "It is too easy to be uncivil when one is so uncomfortable. But I have been thinking about these matters for a long time. I have been forming my resolutions. They are not lightly taken. I was almost ready, in any event, to tell you that I had decided to renounce the domestic life."

"To--?"

"To renounce the domestic life," repeated Clarissa with emphasis. "Homes are an anachronism at the end of the nineteenth century, anyhow. It is time women had the courage of their convictions and sloughed off an anti-social form of habitat that dates from the Stone Age."

"Do you mean you would rather **board?**"

Clarissa stared. "What has boarding to do with it?" she inquired rather haughtily. "I am talking about the universal problem of woman's work. One's own individual makeshifts do not affect that. But if it is ever to be solved, some woman must solve it. Men never will. Sacrifices will have to be made for it, as for other causes. There are women who are ready to make them--and I have discovered that I am one of the women."

Professor Charleroy received this statement in absolute silence.

"As a temporary alleviation," Clarissa went on meditatively, "families might be associated upon some group-system. The operating expenses of the individual establishments would be greatly reduced, and the surplus could be applied to developing the higher life of the members of the group. It would be quite practicable, even in our present crude civilization, to arrange such groups. But of course that would be a temporary expedient. In the redeemed form of social life, it will not be necessary."

"What ails you, Clarissa? Did that lecture you delivered before the Saturday Afternoon Club go to your head?"

Clarissa flushed. Her club paper on "After the Home--What?" was a sensitive subject. She already had been chaffed a good deal about it.

"Of course I know," she said with dignity, "that I am not a genius. I can't organize. I can't write. I'm not pretending to be in the class with Ibsen or Olive Schreiner or Sonia Kovalevsky! No, nor with the American women who are going to work out their ideas. I don't believe I'd make a good social worker, either. I have n't enough patience and tenderness. But I **can** talk. You know I can talk, Paul."

Yes, he knew it. To his cost, he knew it. She had the gift of fluent, winning speech, speech with an atmosphere, a charm. Uncouth theories acquired grace on her lips, and plausible theories seemed stronger than they were. She ironed shirt-waists badly, and the starch stuck to the irons, but she could make the worse appear the better reason with deftness and dispatch. Somewhere, somehow, a coal from the sacred fire had touched her lips. You might be indignant, outraged, at her theories, but you never refused to listen while she set them forth.

"I figure it this way," she continued. "In all great causes, the people who can think and write need the help of the people who can talk, to disseminate their ideas, to popularize them, to get them brought home to the people who don't think and don't read, and yet have influence. That shall be my **métier**. I can do it. I can do it well. I will do it for a living wage and put my heart and soul into doing it. Without going outside a very narrow field,--say, that of parlor talks,--I can yet be a promoter of great causes. I will be a walking-delegate from the Union of the Elect! I will fight the good fight for Utopia! Why, Paul, I can make it glorious!"

Her face shone with a wonderful light. Her slender, delicately rounded figure vibrated with enthusiasm. She did not see the expression on her husband's face. When great thoughts were astir in Clarissa s brain, her high imperturbability, her bright serenity, were maddening. To assail them, logic was as useless as passion. She was simply in another world from this.

Her husband sat down heavily. He felt an unacademic desire to box her ears. Perhaps, had he done so, there would have been no story, for like most women with erratic nerves Clarissa Charleroy had the elemental liking for a masterful man.

However, her husband's Huguenot blood and scholastic training did not help him to carry out such primitive impulses toward domestic discipline. He was a man of sturdy build, with a fine head and brown eyes of the gentle, faithful kind. Conscientious, persistent, upright, he perfectly fitted that old-fashioned description our fathers loved, "a scholar and a gentleman." It cannot be denied that this type is out of place in our modern life; it is especially at a disadvantage when confronted with such a modern wife as his.

"Do you mean to--to *leave* Marvel and me?" he inquired in a voice that was not as even as he could have wished.

His back was toward the window. His wife could not see that he had turned white, but she did notice that he looked steadily down into the palms of his hands.

She faced him with a fine composure.

"I don't see that I'm much good here and I, myself, am certainly very miserable," she said. "There is so much antagonism between you and me, Paul. We think alike about so few things!"

"Do you think the antagonism lies between you and me--or between you and our circumstances?" inquired the professor. His voice was controlled now, but cutting. "Also, do you feel any special antagonism to Marvel? She is rather like yourself, you know."

Clarissa nodded brightly. He was stunned to see that she approved this.

"That's better! Do fight me, Paul! It clarifies my ideas, and I see more definitely what I want. I wish you were a good fighter. I like hard knocks!"

"Good Lord! little girl, you don't mean all this nonsense--you can't. Why, it's impossible. You're my wife. I've done my best. Some day I shall do better. We shall win to peace and comfort yet--if you stand by. My text-book--"

Clarissa waved a disdainful hand. Her blue eyes were liquid, wonderful.

"You don't seem to think of the cause, Paul! Don't you realize that *I can do good work for humanity?* Everybody can't do that. Everybody is n't called to it. I am."

Paul Charleroy let this statement pass. It hung in the air between them, unchallenged, undenounced. Possibly it was true. But, the man was wondering dumbly, what became of other men to whom this thing really happened? Did it crush them all like *this*? How did they keep up hope, decency, honor? How did they preserve their interest in the game and make life worth living afterward? Already he felt heavy upon his heart a presentiment of airless days, of tortured nights. The loneliness of it! No tenderness anywhere in life for him? No love? Then, what use to live? Humanity? Wasn't he humanity?

Nevertheless, when he spoke, he only said, "And Marvel? Is Marvel called to be motherless?"

Clarissa's serene face clouded faintly. The question of Marvel did, indeed, puzzle even her facility. And yet she had light on that problem also.

"If I really prove to be any good,--and I think I shall be a helper in a movement that is going to revolutionize the earth,"--Clarissa said gravely, "there are others to consider besides Marvel. It--why, it ***may*** be, Paul that my duty is to the race! I'm not an especially good mother for Marvel at her present age--the young-animal stage of her development. All a child under twelve years needs is to be properly fed, and clothed, and taught the elementary things. It has all been standardized, and is a matter for experts, anyhow. Your sister Josephine would be a better mother for her for the next few years than I. Why should I do what others can do better? When Marvel begins to ***think***, it will be different. Then she will need my influence. I should like to let you have her for the next few years, and have her come to me when she is fifteen or sixteen. How would that suit you, Paul?"

Her husband moved his shoulders imperceptibly, but said nothing. The thing had passed the point where rational speech, as he conceived it, was in place. If Clarissa did not see the shallowness, the sheer indecency, of discarding one's human relations as if they were old clothes, he could not make her see it. Was it only half an hour ago that he had come down the street in the spring sunshine, under the budding elms, bringing Clarissa a bunch of daffodils and thinking of making a garden, and of all the dear, homely April tasks?

Clarissa assumed that his silence was one of acquiescence. Sooner or later people always acquiesced.

"It is really sweet of you to take it like this, Paul," she said warmly. "I never have understood why people should n't be thoroughly rational about these matters. There's no occasion for bitterness. I should like to have people say we had remained ideal friends. I shall always be as much interested in your welfare as in my own.--Yes, more. I should never dream of marrying again, myself, but in time I think it might be well for you to divorce me and do so." Her mobile face became introspective, absorbed. "Ruth Lawrence is rather too sentimental, not energetic enough for a professor's wife. And Nora Mills is heartless. I think she would marry you for a home, but you must n't let her do it. There is Evelyn Ames. I think Evelyn would do. She is so gentle and reliable!"

She was actually absorbed in this problem, her husband perceived to his utter amazement. He shivered with distaste. This was too grotesque. It could not be true.

His wife looked at him for approval. She noted that the look of fear was gone from his dark eyes. Something unwonted, ironic, flashed there in its stead. It was neither mirth nor malice, yet approached both. He set his boyish-looking mouth firmly, and shook off his silence as one throws off a nightmare. He would meet her on her own ground, and be as indifferent as she.

"Really, Clarissa, **that** is the first sensible thing you have said this afternoon," he forced himself to say.--"Why, what's this?"

It was the small daughter of the house who chose this moment to emerge from under the table, clutching fast a jaded-looking doll and a handful of its belongings. Her round eyes were fear-struck and her quick glance curiously hostile, but she slipped silently from the room. Her presence there was soon forgotten by her parents-- but children do not forget. Of all the incomprehensible words tossed to and fro above her head, Marvel remembered every one.

II

Marvel Charleroy found the letter in the box at the gate where the postman had left it. There was other mail; she glanced at the covers light-heartedly as she went toward the house. She was not very familiar with her mother's handwriting and, for the moment, did not recognize it.

The house was low, gray-shingled, and inviting. It had a kindly, human aspect, and though it was a modern structure built at the time of Professor Charleroy's second marriage, eleven years before, there was about it some thing of that quiet dignity we associate with age. The branches of a wide-spreading old elm swept one of its chimneys; the lawn was broad, the lilacs and syringas tall; ranks of high hollyhocks in shades of rose and wine, rising against gray lattice, shut off the kitchen gardens at the rear. The beds that bordered the paths were planted to a tangle of old-fashioned flowers, gorgeous in the July sunshine. There was a subdued gayety about the whole aspect of the sheltered, sunny place, a look of warmth and home and joy, that was especially dear to Marvel Charleroy. It satisfied in her some elemental need.

She preserved a vivid memory, of which she never spoke, of the box-like little house on Spring Street, her early home. She recalled that house as disorderly and uncomfortable during her mother's regime; as frigid and uncomfortable during the reign of her Aunt Josephine. She figured herself as always holding her breath, as always waiting for something, while she lived there. It was not until she was twelve (four years after Clarissa Charleroy left her husband), that Marvel, to her own childish apprehension, began to fill her lungs, began, indeed, to live.

It will be inferred that the catastrophe, so clearly outlined on that April afternoon fifteen years earlier, did, in fact, occur. For various reasons, it did not take place immediately. For one thing, it required time for Clarissa to put herself into touch with causes that desired to be "promoted" by her silver tongue and wistful, winning ways. Then, too, there were moments when she wavered. So long as Paul could maintain that pose, achieved with great effort, of good-natured, sarcastic scoffing at their tragedy, Clarissa herself did not believe in it wholly. Sometimes they drew very near together. A debonair, indifferent Paul who jested about her "calling" attracted her. A Paul who could demand cheerfully as he took his second cup of coffee, "Well, Clarissa, am I the Tyrant Man this morning?" was not unlikely to elicit the answer, "No, not to-day, Paul. You're just own folks to-day." But a Paul who had heard the wolf howling at the door of his heart, who looked at her with eyes in which she saw fear and the shadow of a broken life, repelled her utterly. Women are reputed to be soft-hearted. Paul Charleroy, musing upon his own predicament in those days, remembered this age-long superstition with wonder.

In spite of various respites, a catastrophe which is latent in a temperament will, some day, come to pass unless, of course, the owner of the temperament decides to be absolute master of himself. Nothing was further from Clarissa's thought than to recapture her married happiness by an assault on her own disposition.

It is not good to linger over this portion of their story. Clarissa did, finally, take over the task of reforming as much of humanity as she could persuade to see the need of it, and she laid aside the business of looking after her husband and her child. Miss Josephine Charleroy, ten years her brother's senior, and competent rather than sympathetic, assumed these discarded responsibilities.

By slow degrees, Paul Charleroy's circumstances became less straitened. He did place his text-book well, and derived a considerable income therefrom; on the death of old Dr. Lettarby he succeeded to the full professorship, with the munificent salary of twenty-five hundred a year. Last of all, some time after Clarissa and he were made free of each other by legal means, he did actually marry Evelyn Ames.

Thus, it will be seen, Clarissa's forecasts were fulfilled. Her notions were absolutely practicable; they really, all of them, worked, and worked well. In the long run they even worked beneficently, but one prefers to attribute this to the mercy of Providence rather than to the foresight of Clarissa.

Marvel Charleroy was twelve years old when her father married again, and life began for her. The little girl noted, dimly at first, then with growing wonder and appreciation, how interesting the commonplace things became under the new rule. Though her frocks were simple as ever, their adaptation to her self made it a pleasure to wear them; she seemed suddenly to have acquired a definite place in the family life, a position with duties and with compensating pleasures. Her friendships were considered, her friends noticed and welcomed. For the first time she felt herself an individual. Somebody was interested in what she did and said and thought. Her own shy young consciousness of personality was reflected back to her, strengthened, and adorned. She perceived with something like awe that the girl named "Marvel" did not live only in her breast. Her father and his wife knew a Marvel whom they believed to be industrious and clever, loving and helpful. These qualities were multiplied tenfold by her perception that they were looked for from that Marvel whom the heads of the house seemed so happy to own and to cherish.

The child throve. She who had wondered vaguely at the stress laid by her books upon the satisfactions of home, now tasted thirstily of that delight. And she repaid the miracle of Evelyn's tenderness with the whole of an ardent heart.

To her elders, the years went fast. Suddenly, as it seemed, Marvel was a young woman with more than her fair share of gifts and graces. She was exquisitely pretty, with an effective little style of her own; she made a brilliant record as a student; she had the rich endowment of easy popularity. Further, she seemed to possess, so far as slight experiments could demonstrate, that rare thing, the genuine teacher's gift. Something of her father's passion for scholarship, something of her mother's silver-lipped persuasiveness, met in the girl and mingled with certain deep convictions of her own.

The practical outcome of all this was the suggestion that her Alma Mater, Midwest, would be glad to attach her to its teaching force without insisting upon an additional degree. She had spent one year abroad since her graduation, part of which was occupied in study. But, like many young Americans, she found her own reflections on the Old World more stimulating than any instruction offered her there.

Now she was at home, ready to begin work in September, enthusiastic, almost effervescent, with her satisfaction in the arrangement of her own little world.

Coming into the shaded house, out of the blaze of the July sunshine, she dropped her father's letters on the desk in his study, and ran upstairs to read her own. It was quite an hour before she heard him calling at the foot of the stair,--

"Marvel! Come down, daughter, I want you."

Something in his voice--she did not know what--gave her a thrill of apprehension. She had never heard just that tone from him before.

She found Professor and Mrs. Charleroy waiting for her in the living-room. Their faces were grave and troubled. Marvel's apprehensive pang mingled with a curious little resentment that her nearest and dearest could allow themselves to look thus, all on a summer morning, in this highly satisfactory world.

"Daughter, I have a letter here," her father began at once, "a letter from your mother. It concerns you more than any one. The question it involves is one for you to decide. I ought not to conceal from you my belief that you will need to consider the matter very carefully."

Marvel took the letter with gravity, hoping that this portentous seriousness was misplaced. This is what she read:--

MY DEAR PAUL,--You remember, of course, that when we separated, it was with the understanding that Marvel was to come to me when she was fifteen or sixteen. But, as you urged, when I brought the matter up at that time, she was then just completing her preparation for college. Since she desired college training, it was certainly easier and simpler for her to have it at Midwest than elsewhere. I put aside my own preferences, because the arguments in favor of her remaining with you were weighty. But it does not seem to me just or right that I should be deprived of my daughter's society entirely, because I waived my preference as to her education. I feel that she has been deprived of my influence, and I of her companionship, already too long.

As I understand it, she graduated a year ago, and has since been abroad. It seems to me this winter will be an excellent time for her to come to me. I shall have an apartment in Chicago, and she will find it easy to arrange for post-graduate work if she desires. I shall be less busy than usual, for my health has given way a little under the strain of my work, and the doctor has warned me to rest as much as possible. I am looking forward with pleasure to introducing her to my friends, my life, my ideas.

When will it be most convenient for her to come? I should say about the first of October.

As ever, my dear Paul, Your sincere friend,

CLARISSA CHARLEROY.

"Well, really!"

Marvel dropped the letter on the floor and turned to face her family with more than a suggestion of belligerence. Her cheeks were flushed, her blue eyes burning, and her head held high with a little air that reminded her auditors swiftly and inevitably of Clarissa Charleroy's self.

"Dear people, what do you look so frightened for?" she demanded. "I call it very cheeky of my mother to make such a demand of me. Does n't she realize that I'm a person with a career of my own--and that when I'm not busy with that, I have to keep my eye on you two! I have n't the slightest intention of leaving home--so you need n't look like **that!**"

Marvel's little harangues usually met with instant response from her family. They were wont to brighten and become argumentative, even when they disagreed. But neither of them answered this pronouncement.

Her father sat by an open window, looking out upon the garden's gayety with unseeing eyes. His wife sat at an other window watching him wistfully, while Marvel faced them both from the hearth, offering her cheerful young defiance for their approval.

Their silence, their gravity, startled the girl. She looked from one face to the other in quick scrutiny. What did this mean? For perhaps the first time in her life, it flashed through her mind that, after all, she knew nothing of the inner attitude of these two people, whom she greatly loved, toward the two facts which had made them all one household--her mother's divorce, namely, and her father's remarriage. The whole structure of three united, happy lives was built upon these cataclysmal facts--yet she had never asked what thought they held of them! Dignified, delicate, scrupulous, she knew them both to be. Through what anguish and uncertainty might they not have passed before they clasped hands at last, making of their two hearts a shelter for her robbed, defenseless one?

Her manner changed on the instant.

"Dear family, you don't ***want*** me to go? Surely--why--you ***can't*** want me to go?"

"No," said Evelyn in a low voice, "dearest, no. Certainly we don't want you to go. Only--"

"But my work!" cried Marvel, passionately, answering their faces, not their words. "I want to do it so much! How can I possibly leave my work? And you, and my life here--everything!"

Her father turned his face farther toward the window, looking out blindly, but Marvel caught his expression--the look of one who tastes again an ancient bitterness. She did not know its full meaning, but her sympathy leaped to meet it. Evelyn Charleroy, watching her, felt a sudden stirring of pride in the girl's swift response to another's need, her quick tenderness. It was thus that Evelyn saw the life of woman--as one long opportunity for the exercise of these qualities.

"Darlingest father, of course I'm not going to leave you. Still, if I were-- what is mother like? What does she expect? What am I to do if I go to her?"

"She is a brilliant woman," answered Professor Charleroy. "In many ways you are not unlike her, Marvel, in mental alertness and all that. As for what she expects--God knows!"

The girl pursued her point. "It is n't an occupation--to be a brilliant woman. I'm not quite sure, even, what she does. She lectures? She is philanthropic, or humanitarian, or something like that? Does she write?"

"No," answered the professor, choosing his words with evident and conscientious care. "That is not her gift. She has the endowment of convincing speech. She has used it admirably for many admirable causes-- and quite as ably for other causes that I esteem less. But that, you understand, is my personal point of view. Her chief interest, however, has been the so-called advancement of women, and you might describe her as one of the many inconspicuous promoters of that movement. Chiefly, at present, she is holding classes, giving parlor-talks, what-not, in which she paraphrases and popularizes the ideas of her leaders. Her personality, though winning, does not carry far, and she is only effective before a handful of people. Her--her conversation is possibly more convincing because it is less susceptible of close examination than the written word. But I do not wish to be unjust."

"Then I take it mother is not scholarly?" asked the girl of academic training.

"She is not taken seriously--by the serious," the professor admitted. "You know, Marvel, there are women who are--who are dearly enthusiastic about the future of the race, who really are not in a position to do advanced thinking about it. Of course there are others of whom I would not venture to make such an assertion, but in my judgment your mother belongs to the former class. You will form your own opinion upon the subject. Do not go to her with any bias in your mind. She is sincere. Her passion for humanity is doubtless real, but it seems to me that her erratic spirit has turned it into a channel where it is ineffective. In any case she is an attractive woman. A winter with her should be interesting."

His daughter eyed him gravely. There were depths of reserve in her face and voice. She had felt much, and said little, about this mother whom they were discussing thus dispassionately. Perhaps it gratified her young dignity that she was able to consider with apparent detachment the woman of whom she had thought long in secret with bitter, blinding tears.

"It is, as you say, a thing to consider," she observed gently. "I may be mistaken in deciding offhand that I will not go. I'll think it over, father dear."

Professor Charleroy rose, visibly pulling himself together. Crossing the room, he picked up the letter Marvel had dropped and handed it to her.

"I also may be mistaken," he said, "in my first feeling about the matter. Yet I think not. But we will not decide hastily."

When he left the room, Marvel partly closed the door and turned to her stepmother.

"Now, Evelyn, you darling, you know all this is perfectly ridiculous. Apparently I can't tell father so,--I could see I was hurting him,--but it simply is ridiculous!"

"I do not feel so, Marvel," Mrs. Charleroy answered steadily.

"What **right** has she?" the girl stormed. "What right, I wish to know? To summon me like this! Didn't she throw us away, father and me, once and for all? You can't recall a thing like that! Why should she think she could take me back any more than father? Influence me, indeed! She does n't know the A B C of influence! I am made--done--finished. Such as I am, she has had no hand in me. If the outcome is creditable, thanks are due to you and father and the Herr Gott. Oh, I know the things that have gone to my making! I don't talk about them much, perhaps, but I know!"

Mrs. Charleroy sat very still, regarding her stepdaughter anxiously. She was a woman of the most benignant of all the elder types: slight, but strong; her brown hair parted smoothly, and brought back from a high full forehead; she had a firm chin, with a tense, sweet mouth, and large, thoughtful, gray-blue eyes.

"Are you quite sure you are completely finished, dear? I would n't dare affirm that of myself."

"If there were no other reasons--why, even if I wanted to go," Marvel went on, "there is my work. I have accepted a position in the English department. They are depending upon me. I am ready, and there is no one to take my place."

"You are mistaken there. Miss Anderson would be glad to retain the position for a year. Something has happened to her arrangements for foreign study, and I heard it intimated the other day that she regretted resigning when she did. She would be delighted to stay on. You could, I think, come back to the position next year. I believe you could arrange with Professor Axtell."

"O Evelyn! Why do you wish to make my going easy? Don't you see I can't bear it?"

"I don't know how to say what I wish," said the elder woman wistfully. "If I remind you that after all she is your mother, I am afraid it will not mean to you what it does to me."

"Certainly I think that, as between us two, the fact no longer carries obligation from me to her!" said Marvel steadily.

"O Marvel! You are hard!"

"No! I am just."

"Justice is never so simple as that," returned Evelyn Charleroy. "But even if it were, your father--I--would rather see you merciful. It would be more like you, Marvel!"

Marvel set the line of her red lips. "I do not wish to go, not even to live up to your idea of me!"

"Marvel, listen to me a moment. I may not be able to make you understand--but I must try. This is the thing I must make you know. The reactions upon the spirit of the ties of the flesh are, simply, the most miraculous things in all this miraculous world. I am not preaching. I am just telling you what I know. This business of being a child, a parent, a husband, a wife,--no creature can escape that net of human relationships wholly. It is there, right there, that we are knotted fast to the whole unseen order of things. What we make of those ties determines what we substantially are. Oh, if you could see it as I see it! This is the real reason, the strongest one of all, for our wishing you to go. You must not throw away the chance it is--the chance of finding out what you are to each other. You must concede something for the sake of learning that!"

"It is n't the mother after the flesh, but the mother after the spirit, to whom are due the great concessions!" cried the girl, "and, Evelyn, ***that*** is you!"

"Marvel--there is still another reason. It may appeal to you more."

Evelyn Charleroy's agitated face, the tumult of her eyes, startled her stepdaughter. She could not bear disturbance of that dear serenity.

"Child!--Do you suppose it was an easy thing for me to come into your father's life and take your mother's place while she still lived? There were months of doubt. There was hesitation that was agony to us both--but in the end--I came. Thus far the thing has seemed to justify itself. It has seemed to work for peace, for blessedness, to us all. I have felt no wrong, have been refused no inner sanction. And yet, I tell you, I am still uncertain of my right to all that your mother threw away, and I do not, even yet, entirely defend my action in taking it! You have been our comfort, our greatest blessing, because it has seemed to be well for you. But, don't you see, if you fail us now; if we have made you selfish; if, through us, you have come to ignore that elemental tie; if you lose out of life whatever it may hold for you, we--we shall doubt our right--we shall be less sure--" The woman's voice fluttered and fell on silence suddenly.

"O Evelyn!" the girl cried out in sharp distress, "don't, don't look like that! Dearest, don't dare to feel like that! There is no need! I won't be horrid! I'll do anything on earth that you and father really wish!"

III

CHICAGO, *November fifth*.

PRECIOUS FATHER AND EVELYN:--

I know all my letters thus far have been rather no-account. They were just to let you know that I was well, and interested, and getting used to things. I loath the city so that I think I must be a country mouse. Every time I go down in the Elevated, past all the grimy, slimy, hideous back buildings, something in me turns over and revolts. I want to be within reach of red leaves, and wheat-stubble, and fat quail running in the roadside grass. Did the little red and yellow chrysanthemums do well this year? How about that marigold border I planted in the kitchen garden?

However, I am going to have a most instructive winter. It was crude of me to think it, but because mother's friends are mostly different kinds of reformers, I expected to find them dubs and scrubs. It seems droll for people who can't live the normal human life successfully to set themselves up to say that therefore it's all wrong, and they will show us a better way to play the game. But only a few of these are that kind of reformers, and they're not dubby and scrubby at all! Some of them are just reformers from the teeth out. They're merely amusing themselves.

Mother is n't playing, however. She's tremendously in earnest. Being a reformer is n't fattening. She keeps back no pound of flesh. She is so thin and tense and nervous, so obsessed with her own ideas, that it worries me some times. I feel as if I lived perpetually in the room with an electric fan. I have been to her classes several times. She has a certain eager eloquence, a real appeal, that will always gain her a hearing. I wish she could keep her neckties straight, but that is a trifle.

Do you remember old Mrs. Knowles saying that she loved to sit at the window and "see the people going pro and con in the street?" That is my present occupation! These people do a tremendous amount of "going pro and con" in the world of the mind. I have been hearing a vast deal of feminist discussion, owing to the appearance of some new books in that line. Can you see why, if nature has spent some thousands of years making women "anabolic, or conservers of energy," they should try to reverse the process in a decade and become even as men, who are "katabolic, or dispensers of energy," just because a stray thinker supposes it would make them more interesting if they all had a business life and dispensed that energy downtown? It seems to me ill-advised to defy nature wholesale. I am willing to work for bread, or for the love of work--but not to oblige illogical theorists!

I'm glad I don't have to reconcile all the different views I hear! One person will argue that woman's work in the home is so complicated and taxing that it all ought to be done for her by specialists, while she goes downtown and becomes some other kind of specialist herself. This is the school of thought to which mother belongs. One or two of its leaders are terribly clever--and mother is rapturously sure that wisdom was born with them! She is so happy to be advocating and expounding their ideas! I find this discipleship pathetic. One does n't deny that they have visions,--mother has them also,--but to me their visions are not divine or beautiful.

The next person will be a reactionary, and say that we are going straight to destruction because some women are thrown into industrial competition with men.

A third will be sure that, because modern life with all its industrial developments outside the home has drawn many women away from home life, therefore all women ought to be thrown out of their homes in a bunch and hustle for themselves in the market-place. There's no longer anything to do at home, and if they stay there they will get fat and lazy and parasitic. I argued about this half the evening with an apple-faced youth of twenty-five who is still supported by his mother. You would have supposed, to hear him, that feminine hands and feet were going to atrophy and fall off from disuse, and that we should turn into some kind of chubby white grub with mouths perpetually demanding to be fed.

I don't deny that there are indolent women in the world, but I certainly never saw any parasites in the college set at Powelton. Somebody will have to "show me" before I can get up any heat of conviction on the subject!

No longer anything to do at home! It has kept me so busy putting one attenuated little reformer-lady's flat to rights and training a cook for her that I have n't had a minute, yet, to see about those courses I meant to take at the University! I shall get around to them presently, I hope.

Mother took the flat before I arrived, and the packers brought her furniture from storage and unpacked it, and set it about according to their fancy, and cleaned up the mess and departed. We moved our trunks out the next morning. Mother went up and down and to and fro, as unsettled as the Cat that Walked. Finally she demanded of me, "Marvel, what ails this flat?" and I said, "Why, mother, the colors are all wrong and it is n't cozy."

She threw up her hands in despair. "Is coziness to be the end of our living?" she demanded; and I said, "It is."

You see, she can explain adorably about beauty in the home, but she had n't known any better than to leave the tinting to the kalsominer.--"Kalsomine is his business. He ought to know better than I," she said. She has such blind faith in specialists.--There resulted a red dining-room, a terrible green living-room, and dark lavender bedrooms! No wonder poor little mother was miserable!

Getting it put right was messy, deplorable, and expensive beyond words; but it is all nice tans now, with charming chintz draperies and chair-covers. I did the upholstering myself, and it is n't half bad.

Mother does n't like ugly things, nor get them of her own free will, but she is obsessed to accept the advice of everybody who pretends to be a specialist, and they "do" her frightfully. It is one of the penalties of being a Superwoman.

Getting a cook required diplomacy. It is a point of honor with mother to take meals in restaurants or buy delicatessen stuff. She was in the hospital two months with inflammation of the liver last winter, and dyspepsia makes half her days hideous. If people will live on indigestible ideas, instead of home cooking, I'm afraid it's what they must expect! I freely admit that I can't combat mother's ideas, as ideas,--I'm not clever enough,--but she does n't know how to be comfortable, which is to be efficient. She is rabidly against kitchens, but arithmetic demonstrates that here, in Chicago, this winter, it will cost less, and be more healthful to have a maid for the season instead of dragging ourselves out in the snow to eat thirty-cent breakfasts and fifty-cent luncheons and seventy-five cent dinners, and pay a woman for coming to clean. I argue that, so long as the Redeemed Form of Society has n't arrived, we are n't disloyal to it by doing this!

Myra Ann has learned to make Evelyn's beef-tea and mutton-broth. Mother needs them badly. Then I discovered that eggs have always disagreed with her, but she went right on eating them because she thought them an "ideal food," and that if her stomach was n't sufficiently standardized to appreciate them, it ought to be! I call that heroic, if it is droll. Idiosyncrasy is something for which mother's creed makes no allowance. We now have an attractive set of eggless breakfasts.--Does all this sound like a model house keeper writing to a domestic journal? Evelyn knows I have a little right to throw bouquets at myself, for I was n't born a housekeeper--but housekeepers **can** be made!

Seems to me, if you ought to standardize an individual's diet, as mother thinks, similar arguments apply to his clothes, his features, his body, his mind, his soul. There's no logical place to stop. Yet we know that diversity, not similarity, is the end nature is always seeking in evolution. Of course, if you are going to buck all the natural laws, that's different!

My country brain gets tired in such a menagerie of ideas. In our own life at home, there is comfort, peace, sufficient stimulus, development; this life is exciting, but barren of something that I will call soil to grow in, because I don't know any better word. Of course it is great fun for me to come in contact with so many different kinds of minds and hear them emit their theories. Only, somehow, the theorists lack reality to me. Do I make myself clear?

I hope this will give you a notion of what I'm doing and thinking, and that you'll know I'm really having a beautiful time. I miss you both horribly, though. I will tell about some of the people in my next letter. I'm acting as mother's secretary just now. She really needs one, and it's interesting work.

Ever and always,

Your loving child, MARVEL.

IV

It was eleven o'clock on a mid-April morning--she never in after-life forgot the day or the hour--that Clarissa Charleroy saw to the depths of her daughter's mind.

Clarissa awoke that morning with a severe neuralgia. She had given two parlor-talks the day before, and was now paying the penalty of overexertion. To lie flat was sickening, yet to rise was impossible.

Marvel promptly took the case in hand. The pillows were piled high; one hot-water bag was slipped under that aching spot at the back of her neck, and another placed at her chilly feet. Marvel knew that a hot bag must be covered with linen; Marvel knew that an alcohol rub changes even a neuralgic's outlook. Marvel was perfectly familiar with the latest non-depressant remedy for neuralgia, hunted up the empty box, telephoned the druggist, and had the prescription filled and ready to administer in half an hour; when she left the room it was only to reappear with a cretonne-and-mahogany tray, fresh toast, and weak tea, at the very psychological moment when the thought of food ceased to be a horror.

Under these ministrations, what had promised to be an all-day siege gave way so satisfactorily that by eleven o'clock Clarissa, arrayed in Marvel's blue negligée, was temporarily reposing on the lounge in the living-room, while her own room was airing. She was in that delicious, drowsy, yet stimulated, state which follows the cessation of suffering.

For April, the day was unusually warm. The windows were open; the sun was pouring happily in, contending in gayety with a great jar of daffodils covering the low table at Clarissa's side. Marvel in a dull-blue house dress, white-braided, sat across the room darning a stocking, with an expression of severity. Mending was one of the domestic duties for which she had little taste. Owing to her constant activities as housekeeper and secretary for Clarissa, she had not yet begun to attend lectures at the University. Her mother, I fear, was serenely blind to the implications of this fact.

Clarissa, lying high among pillows, in the peace that follows pain, regarded her daughter with a profound pleasure. There was something about her--was it the length of curling lashes veiling her eyes? or the tendrils of fair hair the warm wind lifted on her forehead? or the exquisite color that came and went in her cheeks? or the slender roundness of her erect young body?--there was a something, at all events, a dearness, an interest, a charm, unlike all other girls of twenty-three! Not for the first or the second, but for the hundreth time, that winter, Clarissa was conscious of an unutterable hunger for the years she had foregone. She seldom looked at Marvel's bloom without remembering that she had no mental picture of her girlish charm, her maiden magic. How was it possible to grow old without such memories to feed her withering heart upon?

She must not think that the locust had eaten these years! The thought pierced her like a knife, and she put it away from her with all her might. Had she not chosen the better, though more barren, part? Had she not fought a good fight? And for this hour, at least, she was happy.

Leaving Marvel's face, her gaze traveled round the room. The actual alterations were not many, yet they had produced harmony. The apartment was restful now. The very walls seemed to encompass and caress her. Perhaps it was only just, Clarissa reflected, that a woman who had poured out her years and her strength in working and planning for an obdurate world, should have, when her energy was spent, some such warm and tender shelter, some equable spot all flowers and sunshine, wherein she might be tended as Marvel was tending her, so that she might gather strength to go forth to other battles.

She turned her eyes again upon her daughter. Marvel, feeling the long look, glanced up.

"Are you comfy? Is there anything more you want, mother?" the girl inquired.

Clarissa shook her head. "No, nothing. Really, child, you are an excellent nurse. Quite a--quite a Marvel! Were you born so? Where did you get it? Not from Paul or me!"

Marvel smiled faintly to herself.

"Where did I get that name?" she parried. "I have often wondered about that. Father could n't, or would n't, tell me."

The slow, difficult color came to Clarissa's cheeks. How many years since she had recalled the naming of her daughter!

"There is no secret about it," she said. "When the nurse first laid you on my arm, I saw what seemed to me such a wonder-child that I said, Every baby in the world ought to be named Marvel. Mine shall be.-- That's all. It was just a fancy. Your father wanted to name you Clarissa Josephine. Where did those daffodils come from? Did the Herr Professor send them?"

Marvel nodded carelessly. This was so common a matter as to be undeserving of comment.

Clarissa resumed her train of thought. What tact the girl had shown! She had slipped into her mother's life easily. At the beginning she had taken her little stand, assumed her pose. "I am not a believer in your panaceas," her manner always, and her lips once or twice, had said, "but nothing human is alien to me. Pray shatter society to bits and remould it nearer to the heart's desire--if you can."

Clarissa saw no reason why Marvel should not remain with her. A couple of legacies had increased her small income to the point where she might have dispensed with her irregular and uncertain earnings, had these not represented an effort that was the essence of life to her. She could even afford, for a time, the inconsistent luxury of an idle daughter; but if Marvel desired to exercise her teacher's gift, why not do so in Chicago?

"How comfortable we are!" said Clarissa, drowsily and happily. "That blue dress is very becoming to you, child. I believe we can't do better than to keep this flat for next winter. I wonder if we could n't arrange with Myra Ann to come back in the fall? We could pay her half-wages while we were out of town. Her cooking seems to agree with my stomach better than I dared suppose any home cooking could!"

"Why, mother! You forget I am still an instructor-elect at Midwest. I must go to my work in September."

Clarissa started up against her pillows and spoke with her usual vehemence and directness.

"I do not wish you to go back to Midwest, Marvel. I want you to stay with me. I have had too little of my daughter's society in my life."

The girl dropped her work and faced her mother. "That, mother, is hardly my fault."

Their glances met and crossed, rapier-like, with the words. Apprehension seized Clarissa. She did not fathom the meaning of Marvel's gaze.

"Do you mean it is my fault, Marvel?"

Her daughter kept silence. For almost the first time in her life, the older woman felt herself compelled to valiant self-defense.

"My work has justified itself, Marvel. I am not boasting when I say that I truthfully believe the good day of release from servitude is nearer for all women because I had the courage to leave my home and go into the wilderness, preaching the coming of the Woman's Age and furthering, even though feebly, all the good causes that will help it on."

Marvel still kept silence. She knew so many things to say! Was it not better to utter none of them?

"I wanted," continued Clarissa, "to give my mite toward making this a better world for girl-babies like you to be born into."

Her face wore the deep, wistful look that marked her highest moments; this was the reason upon which in her secret soul she relied for justification--but her daughter was not touched by it at all!

"Well, Marvel?"

"Really, mother," said the girl crisply, driven to make answer, "don't you realize that you would never have gone in for Humanity if you had n't hated cooking?"

"Why cook when I hated it?" Clarissa, up-in-arms, flashed back.

"Why, indeed?--but why drag in Humanity? And why should I give up my work to stay here? I felt I ought to come--for a while--when you asked it. I could see that father and Evelyn thought I ought. But now that I have put the flat in shape and trained Myra Ann,--she wants to stay with you, by the way,--things will run smoothly. I can come up occasionally to see how it goes."

At this assumption that her need of her child was purely practical, something, some tangible, iron thing, seemed to strike Clarissa's heart. She could feel its impact, feel the distressful shudder along all her nerves, the explosion in her palms. She looked down at them curiously. It almost seemed to her that she would behold them shattered by the pain!

She turned her eyes away and they fell upon the bowl of daffodils. Daffodils burning in an April sun. In what long-forgotten hour of stress had she once seen the flame of daffodils burn bright against an April sun? Slowly her brain made the association. Ah, yes! That day she told Paul she would leave him, he had brought her daffodils.--Had **Paul** felt like this?

Clarissa--Clarissa who had never before either asked or given quarter--heard her own voice, tense with feeling, say, "Marvel, I can't let you go, not yet!"

"Why, mother! I can't stay longer than June. Of all people in the world, you ought to admit that I must do my work! Of course I know you need a home as much as any one, though you never own it. That's why you have liked to have me here this winter because I could help you make one. You none of you know, you reformers! You are just air-plants. You have no roots."

"It is part of the profession. 'Foxes have holes--'" Clarissa retorted, driven to her last defense.

Marvel lifted her head, shocked at the implication.

"I don't believe it is wrong to tell you what I think," she said abruptly. "You ought to know the other side, my side. Of course I'm only a girl still. I dare say there is a great deal I do not understand. But I do know about homes. The attitude of these people you admire and quote does seem to me so ridiculous! They all admit that the race lives for the child. But they say--and you follow them--that the child can be best cared for by specialists, and the house can be left to itself, while the mothers can, and should, go out and hunt up some other specialty. It is the idea of a shirk! Loving a child is a profession in itself. You have to give your mind and soul to it. I tell you I know. *I know because I was motherless!* Can't you see that everything your specialists can do for the child is useless if you don't give it what it wants and needs the very most of all? Oh, I think some grown-ups were born grown-up. They don't seem to remember!"

"Remember--remember what?" Clarissa interjected sharply.

"I don't know that I can make you understand. It is such a simple, elemental thing. You either know it, or you don't. You may mother chickens in a brooder, but you must mother children in your arms. After you left, mother, for four mortal years I was the most miserable scrap on earth. I was fed and clothed and taught and cared for. I was petted, too, but it was never *right*. All the while I felt myself alone. Aunt Josephine did n't count; even father did n't, then. I could not sleep for loneliness, and I used to wake far in the night, my eyes all wet with tears. I had been crying in my sleep. The universe felt desolate and vacant. Just one little girl alone in it! There was such a weight at my heart! I would cry and cry. It was an awful, constant hunger for the mother that I did n't have. So I know how it is with all children. Their hearts must be fed!"

Clarissa listened, astounded.

The girl stood now at the open window, breathing in the soft spring air in long-drawn, tremulous breaths. The excitement of speech was upon her. Her eyes were liquid, wonderful. And never, in all her life, had she looked so like the woman who watched her breathlessly.

"These are such big things," she went on, "I hardly know how to talk about them. But I have thought a great deal. I know the world must be made better, and every one must do his share. But, mother, you can't save the world in platoons. Even Christ had but twelve disciples. I'm not denying that thousands of women must work outside the home; I'm not denying that hundreds may be specially called to do work in and for the world. But the mothers are not called. They must not go, unless want drives. They have the homes to make--the part of the homes that is atmosphere. Oh, don't you know what I mean? The women who understand can make a home in a boarding-house or in foreign lodgings; in a camp on the desert or in an eyrie in the mountains. It's the feel of it! Don't you understand it at all,--the warm, comforted, easeful feeling that encompasses you when you come in the door, or raise the tent-flap? Home is the thing that nourishes, that cherishes, that puts its arms about you and says, Rest here!

"I know--for father and Evelyn made a home for me. Father is like me. He is lost, shipwrecked, ruined, if his heart is n't sheltered. I don't know what I think about divorces and re-marriages. It is all so perplexing. I do not know at all. But I know you broke up a home, and Evelyn made one. Whatever people do, if they can do that for a child as father and Evelyn did it for me, I should n't wonder if they are justified before gods and men!"

The rapid sentences fell like hammer-strokes upon Clarissa's naked heart. She felt that she ought to be defending her beliefs, but she could not take her eyes from Marvel's glowing face, and the girl went swiftly on:--

"The people that you follow--they admit the race lives for the child, that the mother must risk her life to give it life. Then, they seem to think, the sacrifice can cease. But if you know about homes, you know better. As she gives her body to be the matrix of another body, so she must give her spirit to make a shelter that shall be the matrix of another spirit. If she refuses to do this, she fails, and all her labor is in vain. It is very simple. As I see the world, the mothers must die daily all their lives. There is no other way. It is a part of life, just as bearing and birth are parts of life. No one denies that they are hard--hard--hard. But that is the glory of it! Nothing is worth while that lacks the labor and the danger, the pain and the difficulty!"

For once in her life Clarissa was speechless. Words would not come. The inherited weapon of her own fluency had been turned against herself. For as other women had been shaken from their old faiths and allegiances by Clarissa's gift of tongues, even so had she been shaken by her child. The girl's young cogency had struck her dumb.

In the long minutes of silence that followed, Clarissa was, perhaps, more truly a mother than she had been since Marvel first lay in the circle of her arm. She saw a daughter's point of view at last. She knew which proclaimed the deeper doctrine, which was the truer prophet of humanity, her child or she.

Yet when she spoke at last, it was not to discourse of Humanity. Humanity was forgotten; she and her child were all. Her lips shaped, unbidden, that old, old demand of the hungry heart.

"Marvel--don't you *love* me at all?"

Marvel hesitated. Her air of detachment was complete.

"You never tried to make me love you, mother. Even love goes by a kind of logic. Domestic life gives you one kind of reward; public life another kind. You get the kind you choose, I take it, and no other. If you want love, you must choose the love-bringing kind," said this austere young judge. "And I've found out another thing by myself. You love ten times as much when you have served with hands and feet as well as brain. I do not know why. I only know you do. If--if I love you at all, mother, it is because of the work I have done for you here--in making it like home!"

Clarissa bowed her head on her hands, in a bitterness made absolute. This child of hers was her own child. What right, indeed, had she to expect self-sacrifice, tenderness, cherishing, from the flesh of her flesh? That which she had given was rendered unto her again in overflowing measure, and beholding she saw that it was just.

Marvel, standing at the window in the sunshine, a little excited by her own eloquence and wondering at it still, had no conception of the havoc she had worked. Indeed, she was innocent of the knowledge that any one, least of all herself, had the power to move her mother greatly. She assumed, after the careless fashion of youth, that her elders were indifferent and unemotional. Suddenly, she heard an unfamiliar and terrifying sound. Her mother was sobbing with harsh, rending sobs, tearless and terrible.

Marvel turned in quick alarm and stood confused before this anguish of her own inflicting. Clarissa's very soul seemed sobbing, and her daughter did not know how to bear the sound.

The girl wrung her hands helplessly. Something struck her heart and quivered down her nerves. Then, as she watched this woman, so like, yet so unlike herself, all at once--she understood! She was suffering with every painful breath her mother drew. In the heart of her heart she felt them. They two were bound together there. It was even as Evelyn had told her,-- Evelyn, the beloved, whose truth had never failed her yet! The primal tie that draws God to his worlds still holds the woman and her child. It was a wonder and a miracle unspeakable--but it was true. Throbbing and palpable, she felt the tie.

It was as if her eyelids were anointed, and all the deep and secret things of life lay clear. Ah, she had not known the half before! How shallow and complacent she must have seemed! She dropped on her knees beside the lounge. No eloquence now! She stammered commonplace words eagerly, pitifully.

"Mother dear! Mother, I didn't mean to hurt you so! I did n't know. ***I did n't know!*** Don't cry! O mother dear, ***don't cry!***"

Clarissa lifted a drawn, woeful face, and looked straight into her daughter's eyes. I cannot tell you what she saw there of wonder and newborn tenderness. But she drank of that look thirstily, as might one who had found springs of living water after a desert drought.

Her own child's hand had struck her down. Yet, in her overthrow, she read in Marvel's face the sign all mothers seek. Ungentle and unmerciful the girl had been, yet gentler and more merciful than she! And by that token she knew her life not wasted utterly. For she had given to this world--this piteous world for which she had labored clumsily and ineffectually in alien ways--the best thing that the woman has to give. Offspring a little better than herself she gave to it. This child of hers, just now so hard, yet now become so pitiful, was her own child and more. Of her flesh and of her spirit had been wrought a finer thing than she.

Milton Keynes UK
Ingram Content Group UK Ltd.
UKHW050242220624
444555UK00005BA/475

9 789362 093264